The Voice of Coyote

and Other Spirit Animal Tales

Doug Hodges (signature)

as told to Doug Hodges

To Terry —
old & pleasant ghosts
may the spirits watch over you
& keep you ever moving
may you enjoy!
Peace!
Doug
1/2005

This book is a work of fiction. Places, events, and situations in this story are purely fictional. Any resemblance to actual persons, living or dead, is coincidental.

© 2003 by Doug Hodges. All rights reserved.

No part of this book may be reproduced, stored in a retrieval system, or transmitted by any means, electronic, mechanical, photocopying, recording, or otherwise, without written permission from the author.

ISBN: 1-4107-4496-5 (e-book)
ISBN: 1-4107-4495-7 (Paperback)

Library of Congress Control Number: 2003092417

This book is printed on acid free paper.

Printed in the United States of America
Bloomington, IN

1stBooks - rev. 07/21/03

this book is dedicated to all those
who have seen me on my way
whose Spirits have touched my own
and, in turn, allowed mine to touch theirs
all who could never dream of where I am today
all who despaired that I ever had a path and gave up
all who never gave up and believed

Doug Hodges

Introduction

sometimes, it seems so long ago
    sometimes, only yesterday
that I went on my Quest in the Big Bend of Texas
there, Raven came to me
    and asked me to change my life
he told me that if I were to
    have faith the Spirits would guide me
        and keep me safe
I did and they have …
I quit my job, sold most of what I owned
    left the mountains of Colorado
        and took to the road,
            covering some 60,000 miles
eventually, love brought me to the Rio Grande Valley
    where I have settled
here, my journey continues …

the Spirits have given me many tales
mostly from Coyote, who likes to talk
    and who, perhaps in me, found a kindred spirit
in order to better share these tales
    I self-published three volumes of poems,
        songs & stories
    Coyote/Wolf: canines in transition
    Raven: more tales of Spirit Animals
    Coyote: The Newer Tails
from those, and with stories not yet printed,
    come this compilation

*the Great Spirit watch over you all
wher'er you trod your path
and bring you peace*

great bear and coyote was originally self-published in <u>24 Poems: Odyssey</u>, 1997
Coyote Stuffing was previously printed in <u>The Modern Rhapsode</u>
October-November, 2000, Brownsville, TX
Texas Wolf won 3rd Place for short fiction in the
2002 Valley ByLiners Excellence in Writing contest, La Feria, TX

The order in which they've been given:

Great bear and coyote - September 18, 1995 1

Afternoon jive - March 4, 1997 2

Coyote and Raven - October 28, 1997 5

Coyote As The Dinner Guest - January 25, 1998 6

Coyote and the Pie - January 25, 1999 9

Raven and Coyote - January 26, 1998 12

Coyote on the Beach - April, 1998 14

The Muddy Waters of the Platte - July, 1998 16

Raven and the Soul - August 6, 1998 19

Coyote and The Tooth - September 29, 1998 20

A Death Of Coyote - November 25, 1998 22

Coyote Visits Rabbit and Raven - December 15, 1998 24

Grandfather Buffalo's Lesson - December 24, 1998 28

Coyote In The Night - January 27, 1999 30

Coyote Sings - February, 1999 33

Coyote and the Wind - March 29, 1999 35

Storm - June 7-17, 1999 37

The Dolphin and the Pelican - June, 1999 39

A Lesson In Stuffing - July-August, 1999 41

Coyote and the Cowboy - August 27, 1999 46

Texas Wolf - September 15, 1999 49

Coyote and the Traveling Companion - October 13, 1999 51

Coyote On the Island Or Coyote and the Great Blue Heron - Fall, 1999 53
Coyote Along The Border - November 17, 1999 55
Coyote and the Angel - November 23, 1999 58
Coyote As The Teacher - November 20, 1999 60
A Christmas Along the Rio Grande - Christmas, 1999 62
Coyote and The Cross - March, 2000 71
'Foxy' Morning - April 6, 2000 74
Coyote's Plan - May 11, 2000 77
Coyote at the Hospital - June 8, 2000 78
The End of The River - February 15, 2001 80
Coyote and Roadrunner - August 8, 2001 82
An Unkindness Of Ravens - November 23, 2001 84
Coyote Goes To Heaven - June, 2002 87
Coyote And The Favor or What's A Miracle Between Friends - July, 2002 90
Idioms - August 29, 2002 93
War Clouds - October 8, 2002 96
Coyote and The Prophet - January 16, 2003 98
The Faithful Companion, Coyote - February 22, 2003 100

The Voice of Coyote

great bear and coyote

Great Bear of the woods loudly proclaims, "I am legend."
he stands upright and waves his huge paws
towering far above little Coyote who seems
to be but half listening, preoccupied with his fleas
"Man fears the very mention of *my* name!"

Coyote finally looks up and says,
"Yet, you are almost extinct …
Your name will outlive your very existence."
He smiles and quietly goes on,
"You are tied to the woods. You are big but have few babies.
Man hunts you for sport and out of fear.
I live everywhere, in wood and desert,
on farms and in cities.
I have big litters. I am legion.
Man hunts you and you die, slowly but surely.
Man kills me and I live on and on."

Great Bear stands pondering
the sun throws his great shadow over Coyote
one last time, Coyote bites a raggedy haunch
overflowing with fleas
then, he smirks, turns his back on Bear
and walks away into the sunlight

September 18, 1995

as told to Doug Hodges

afternoon jive

getting little done … but done so well
after a day's work, I withdrew
from that place, with fortune in hand
I started on foot down the dusty road

I first met Coyote, sitting on a stump
He gave me a name, but wouldn't
Tell me what he wanted in return
And we all know coyote always wants something

a little troubled in my mind, I
nevertheless continued, feet kicking up dust,
which the wind blew 'round and 'round
when out of the swirling dust came Raven

Raven offered to give me direction
and then asked me for my name
I gave him the name Coyote had given me
and explained that Coyote had asked for nothing in return

Raven cocked his head; he knew what Coyote wanted
and he told me what to do
he said I must be very swift and cunning
for Coyote was out collecting souls

I would meet Coyote again, Raven said
and would be asked my name
I was to pretend to have forgotten
and make Coyote utter it first

it was a moon later and I was enjoying my name
spreading it through the windy and dusty villages
when an old women met me at a crossroads
I could see behind the face, in her eyes, that it was Coyote

She said, "I have heard from all the women

The Voice of Coyote

that you have a fine name,
but I can't remember what it was.
Please tell me so that I may tell my daughters."

I replied, "Yes, it is a fine name,
but sometimes I have a hard time remembering it.
Let me think …" "Oh, come," said Coyote
"surely you can remember your own name."

"Well," I said, "I haven't had it all that long …
Could it be …" and gave a number of
similar sounding names
"No, no!" screeched Coyote, "Those can't be right."

"For a fine young man such as yourself," Coyote continued
"it could only be something wonderful, powerful.
Try again … think, rolling the syllables around your tongue.
Hurry! I am anxious for my lovely daughters
to know who you are."

I tried again and again, narrowly missing the name
Coyote danced around in frustration
"You idiot, numbskull …
How could you forget such a simple name?"
Coyote wrung his hands and tore at his old woman's hair

"Maybe it sounds something like …" and he started the name
"That feels very familiar ..." said I, then ended it improperly
"No, no! Imbecile, cretin! What's the matter with you?
It's …" and Coyote shouted the name, three times actually

Coyote stopped, looked at me, and knew he had lost
"How did you know?" the old woman muttered, "How?"
the old woman then melted into the figure of Coyote
shining and brazen as ever

"There will be other times, other games." Coyote said
and was gone with the swirling dust
Coyote hates to lose, but he does

as told to Doug Hodges
    about as often as he wins

March 4, 1997

Coyote and Raven

It happened that Coyote was walking down a dusty road one day when he came upon Raven who was munching on a deer carcass. Now, Coyote was hungry and, believing he was the smartest of all creatures, figured there had to be a way to get the aromatic meal away from Raven. After all, Raven was only a bird, and a plain black one at that.

"You know," began Coyote, "that carcass must be full of disease and it's dirty. Now," placing a friendly arm around Raven's shoulders, "I just passed a freshly killed boar just the other side of this hill. I would have eaten it myself but I had a late lunch."

"I know you, Coyote." replied Raven "You just want to get my meal. I also know you are always hungry."

"No! Honest!" exclaimed Coyote. "It's there. I'm always so maligned. I'm just trying to do you a favor. If you don't want it, fine. No skin off my behind. I'm sure I'll meet someone a bit more trusting on down the road." And, Coyote walked off, trying to look nonchalant.

Now, Raven wasn't born yesterday but his pickings were a bit gamy, so he said, "Coyote, if I fly over the hill to take a look, will you watch my meal here? You're really not hungry, you say?"

"No, I'm not. Sure, I'll watch this. You never know when some scumbag will come along and take some honest person's dinner. But, I promise, you won't be back when you see what's over there."

So, Raven flew off, and Coyote, feeling proud of himself, drug off the remains of the deer, chuckling at the stupidity of the world in general and black birds in particular.

Raven flew over the hill and found the freshly killed remains of a large boar. He called his family over for the feast and dug in, thinking all the while, what a great guy Coyote was.

October 28, 1997

as told to Doug Hodges

Coyote As The Dinner Guest

Coyote was bored; same o'le, same o'le.
Rabbit had been after him to come to dinner.
He liked Rabbit, so he called her up.
"Rabbit! This is Coyote. How are you? Yes, I'm fine. I've been busy; just doin' stuff. I thought I'd take you up on your dinner invitation., if it's still open. That's great! Anytime's fine with me. Tomorrow evening, six o'clock. I'll be there. Do I need to bring anything? Ok. No, I won't eat anything before I come. I've missed you, too. Bye!"

"Great!" thought Coyote, with anticipation. He knew Rabbit was a vegetarian, hence the 'don't eat anything before' comment, but what the heck, vegetarians don't starve and he really did like Rabbit.

He had spent a night with her at a Stones' concert a number of years back, nestled together in a sleeping bag in a ditch beside Horsetooth Reservoir. They'd been friends ever since, seeing each other frequently, though they hadn't actually gone out together.

So, the next day Coyote polished up his old grey pickup with a dirty shirt, taking care not to rub off his '78 Bronco sticker, brushed his teeth and fur, and set out for Rabbit's.

She lived in a quaint dome house down where the foothills met the plains. The house was pretty and neat, with a small green lawn, much neater than Coyote's ramshackle mountain cabin. Well, after all Rabbit was female and neatness seems to go with the territory.

At the door, they kissed cheeks and in he went. Something smelled good on the stove and he commented on it. She thanked him, "That's the stew." Then, she asked if he wanted any tea. He replied, "No thank you." She said, "Make yourself at home." and ambled off into the kitchen.

Coyote sat down on a futon and looked around. Home was never like this. The room was tastefully full of flowers in planters and plants hung from the ceiling.

Pictures were spaced evenly around the walls: landscapes, an old rabbit. Every inch of Coyote's cabin walls were full of calendars, photos, posters, maps, newspapers, clippings, bills, anything he took a notion to stick there at the time.

Rabbit had a neat little coffee table ('I'll bet she never drinks coffee off it,' Coyote thought), holding a couple of large books full of pictures of far away places and not much writing.

On one wall was a small bookcase. With a grunt, Coyote got up and looked at the titles: health, yoga, women's issues, self-help. "My Louis L'Amours sure wouldn't fit in here," he murmured.

Sitting back down, he noticed the cleanness of the room. Not that his cabin was dirty, but it was full. Full of his stuff. Every nook and cranny seemed to grow something of interest to him. That made him comfortable. But, everything he had seemed to perpetually acquire dust.

This room was neat, immaculate; like something out of a magazine.

Rabbit came in, "Dinner's ready, Coyote."

"Stew!" she said again as she placed a large pan in the center of the kitchen table. "What would you like to drink?"

Coyote, who wanted nothing more than a beer at that moment, had to think. Okay, Rabbit doesn't drink; I know that. "Do you have any soda pop?" he asked.

"Yes, I have some natural soda, heavily sweetened, that I bought just for you. I drink naturally flavored waters."

"Oh, that's great," said Coyote. "Ya got orange?"

"Yes." smiled Rabbit; "I remembered your favorite."

The stew wasn't bad, Coyote thought. There was something in it that seemed suspiciously like meat, but he was assured that it wasn't. The bread was excellent and he had three thick slices with his two bowls of stew. Imagine, no sugar, no preservatives, no milk, no egg, no anything that the basic world deems necessary for survival.

After dinner, he thought a bottle of wine would have been perfect. They sipped Celestial Seasons herb teal; hers was Emperor's Choice, his was a spiced orange. "Have you thought about becoming a vegetarian?" Rabbit asked.

Coyote almost choked. He thought, 'Have I thought about cutting my throat?'

"No," he replied. "I haven't thought much in that direction."

"Well," she went on, "It's healthy and purifies the body and the spirit."

as told to Doug Hodges

With that, they discussed the old Stones' concert, mutual friends, times good and bad, and after an hour or so, she asked, "Would you like to go to bed?"

Coyote would have choked again but he had finished his tea by this time.

He looked at Rabbit and she was every bit as cute and desirable as she had been that night so long ago (though, truth be known, he had been flying on peyote at the time). He could feel desire rising in him.

"Thanks Rabbit, but I can't. Possum and I are leaving very early in the morning to cut wood; laying in supplies for ourselves and the neighbors for the coming fall and winter. I really do appreciate the offer."

"I'd better be going, as a matter of fact. Thanks for a great dinner … a great time, Rabbit."

Coyote kissed Rabbit on the lips and they waved their good-byes. He got into his truck and drove off. The night seemed to have acquired a chill.

'Must be getting old,' he thought. 'I'll have to remember and call Possum when I get home and tell him we're cutting wood in the morning. He'll like that!"

Coyote wondered if there would be a MacDonald's open along the way.

January 25, 1998

Coyote and the Pie

One day, Old Grandmother Sunwoman baked two wild cactus pies which smelled of strawberry and mesquite. The delicious smell spread from the flat rocks upon which they were cooling to the nostrils of Coyote, who happened to be walking a path near by.

Drawn by the scent, he peered through a thicket of cactus trees, at first seeing only the painted mountains of Mexico rising in a sheer escarpment as they lay across the Big River.

Then, he saw Old Grandmother Sunwoman go into her tee-pee; then his nose drew his eyes to the pies. 'Oh,' he thought, 'I must have one. After all, she baked two.' It was not in Coyote's nature to ask Old Grandmother Sunwoman for one, which she may have freely given; it was in his nature to sneak one. Just one, for Coyote was not greedy and would never take more than he could eat.

So, creeping through the thistle and cacti, consoling himself at each prick and gouge with the mouthwatering thought of pie, Coyote moved steadily closer.

Only to find himself, at the very brink of success, with one paw hovering over a pie, staring eye to eye with Old Grandmother Sunwoman.

Arising from his slouch, trying to achieve some sense of dignity, Coyote said, "Ah, Old Grandmother Sunwoman, all honor to you on such a lovely day. I couldn't help but notice that you've been baking. And, your pies smell absolutely delicious."

"So," Old Grandmother Sunwoman replied, "You would steal one."

"Oh, no!" protested Coyote, "I was just so entranced by the aroma that I must have forgotten myself. But, I was going to call out to you. Really!"

"Well," Old Grandmother Sunwoman looked dubiously upon Coyote, "I do have two pies. However, one is an eating pie, full of juices and good tastes. One is a medicine pie, full of magic; from a recipe that Raven has given me.

Now, Coyote wanted no truck with magic. And, he had had dealings with Raven before, an altogether untrustworthy individual.,

"Honored grandmother," he said, "Could I please have a piece of the eating pie?"

as told to Doug Hodges

Old Grandmother Sunwoman, still looking somewhat askance upon Coyote, suddenly smiled and said, "I'll tell you what. I'll cut a piece from each pie and you can choose one between them."

Coyote sat down, scratched behind one ear, and thought, 'Well, a piece of pie is better than no pie at all. But, what would the magic pie do to me?'

"Honored Grandmother, I am honored and accept your kind offer. Just one small question, what will the magic pie do?"

"Why," Old Grandmother Sunwoman replied, "Whatever you think."

'Whatever I think …' thought Coyote. 'How bad can that be?'

By this time, two large slices of the delicious smelling pies lay on a shallow clay bowl in front of Coyote. He hesitated, grabbed the left one and gobbled it up.

First, a sweet sensation filled his stomach. His cheeks bulged out. His face and fur turned a bright yellow, like the rising sun. Coyote blew up like a big yellow balloon and he just managed to roll over on his back when, like Beetle, he could move no more.

After a while, a fire began in the pit of his stomach and came forth to scald his lips and flow, a raging flame, through his veins. Coyote returned to his original size, stumbled to his feel and, this time, turned as red as a blooming cactus flower. He couldn't catch his breath and just stood there, swaying, a sort of whistling coming from his mouth, ears, and rear end.

After a while, the taste of dirt filled his mouth … of blackened trees and death. Fear gripped Coyote as his body turned black and all sensation left him. He would have trembled but that he was dead inside.

After a while, the taste in his mouth grew tart. Coyote's lips pursed and he shook himself. He grew pale, so pale that he was whiter than sandstone.

After a while, Coyote returned to his normal coloring. After checking his fur and appearance, which seemed to be okay, Coyote sat down with a thump. "Wow!" was all he could say.

"Thank you Honored Grandmother." Said Coyote, finally recovered. "Next time I am passing through, I'll be sure to holler out and ask you for a piece of your delicious pie."

With that, coyote turned and walked away, not quite as sure of step nor as perky as when he had first come, thinking to himself, 'But not for a long, long, long, long, time.'

January 25, 1998

as told to Doug Hodges

Raven and Coyote

Raven and Coyote were neighbors, distant neighbors. They didn't associate much with each other for each was a trickster; each had magic.

But, occasionally the path of life brought them together as on this sunny morning one January in the Big Bend country.

Raven was sitting high in a cactus tree. He was bored.

"You know, Friend Coyote, there are some fat sheep across the Great River, there."

Coyote looked up, "Oh!" He was also bored and getting hungry.

"Why, yes!" said Raven. "I see a place where you could swim across, not too far, not too swift, not too deep, and come up upon them unawares."

"And, why are you telling me this, Friend Raven?" asked Coyote, dubiously.

"Just being neighborly." replied Raven.

"There aren't any herders or dogs?" asked Coyote.

"Nary a one." answered Raven.

"Okay, tell me where the crossing is." And Raven did.

Coyote was half-way across the Rio Grande, the painted hills of Mexico rose before him, when he felt a curious sensation. He was tiring. That shouldn't be. The way across had been but a hundred feet. And, curiously, now that he thought about it, the other side seemed to be getting no closer, no matter how much he swam.

Coyote began to become anxious and he suspected some trick.

Raven flew overhead. "Is the way too long and hard, Friend Coyote? Are we getting a little too old for a short swim?"

Coyote, whose legs by this time were very tired, and it was all he could do just to keep his head above water, managed to reply, "What trickery is this? I'm no closer than half-way to either shore, no matter how hard I swim."

"Oh!" said Raven, "Didn't I tell you? That's the Guardian Hole of the River. From the center, where you are, you can never get to one side or the other."

"Great!" said Coyote. "And, I suppose you expect me to just swim here forever."

The Voice of Coyote

"That thought had occurred, yes." said Raven. And, with a proud kawwk-cackle, he flew away across the escarpment and into the sun.

"Well, fiddle-de-de!" said a chagrined Coyote, who by this time could no longer stay afloat. Of course, he could use magic to stay up, but if he was going to use magic, he'd do it more effectively.

He sank to the bottom of the river, beneath the Guardian Hole of the River, and finished his way across, walking.

On the other side, he found the sheep and finding one to his liking, after giving thanks to the Great Spirit and to the spirit of the sheep, Coyote made a well-earned meal.

Full and rested, Coyote chuckled at Raven's trick. He said to himself, 'I'll have to remember that nothing is what it seems around Raven. We'll just see what happens the next time we meet.' And, Coyote laughed and laughed 'til it seemed his sides would split.

January 26, 1998

as told to Doug Hodges

Coyote on the Beach

One bright morning, Coyote found himself at some small white hills. They were semi-weeded and at first looked like the snow-covered hills of New Mexico. But, upon closer inspection, he found the white to be sand.

Realizing that nothing happens by chance, he ambled over the hill to see what could be seen. Here, an amazingly white expanse of sand let out onto a gently lapping sea, a gulf actually, but still an expanse of water drifting as far to the horizon as the eye could see.

Raised voices brought Coyote down onto the beach where he came upon two birds discoursing on the palatability of different types of fish. One of these was a normal looking bird, to Coyote's way of thinking. It was white, with grey markings and a tilted beak. The other was very different, indeed. Although, it too was white, the resemblance ended there. This one stood horizontal like a human and it had a large orange sack beneath its beak. Coyote sat and watched for a while. When it appeared the birds had paused to take a breather, he introduced himself.

The more normal-looking bird spoke first and said that it was called a seagull, "Call me Seymour, everyone does."

"I ride the ocean currents and soar high and wide across the sea, often days or weeks from shore. I dine with sailors on the briny main, fellow creatures who have given their souls to the sea."

"Quite eloquent," said the other bird, "for a scavenger that eats anything." He turned to Coyote, "I am a pelican. I eat fish and can store a great deal in this pouch beneath my bill. I sit on posts way out there in the water and look awfully picturesque."

"I eat fish, too." said the miffed seagull, which had been preening itself while Pelican spoke.

'Here's a chance to have some fun.' thought Coyote. "So, mister pellicum, how big is that sack anyway?"

"That's pelican, C-A-N." replied the bird. "It's incredibly large. I can live for a terribly long time on the fish stored there. I can haul large amounts great distances."

"Is that so?" said Coyote. "Could I take a look?"

"Harrumph! I suppose so." And the pelican opened his great bill.

The Voice of Coyote

Coyote peered down in. "Humm … hummmm … Seymour, take a look. Isn't that a piece of fish stuck down there … at the bottom?"

The seagull flew up and grabbing hold of the pelican's bill leaned over and stuck his head down and in. An, "I believe so," echoed up out of the depths of the pelican's pouch. "I'd better go down and retrieve it. He probably doesn't even know it's there it will just rot and give him gas and bad breath."

With that the seagull let go of the sides of the pelican's bill and was completely inside. The pelican said, "Arrwwgghh!"

Coyote grinned. The pelican tried to speak again, "At, awwnn awn?"

Coyote sidled up to the pelican, "You know," he said in a soft voice as he ran a claw gently down the pelican's wing, "I've been known to eat birds."

The pelican's eyes widened. He snapped his bill shut, to a muffled, "Hey!" from inside. The pelican ran down the beach flapping his wings. Taking a few steps longer than if he had no passenger, he was aloft and flapping out to sea for all he was worth.

Coyote roared with laughter and rolled around in the sand until he was as white as the pelican had been, the fine sand finding its way into every crease and working into the fur so that it'd take forever to get clear. And coyote laughed at that, also.

April, 1998

as told to Doug Hodges

The Muddy Waters of the Platte

The river roamed drunkenly across the high plains as Coyote followed. He was wary because in a moment, this wet sandy bog could explode into a raging torrent of water. Yet, the Platte was the road west and the easiest followed.

Early, or late, well before sunrise, Coyote came to a crossroads; just a dirty 'X' in the road with an abandoned gas station on one side and a small square diner on the other. From the diner's windows came a welcoming light and Coyote pulled his battered gray pickup into the dirt lot. There was a flashy red sports car of some sort also parked there. Half-hidden behind the building, an old rusted panel truck, one of those with an Indian name, Coyote thought, could be seen trying to hide.

The inside was cheery if not altogether clean; a row of stools, covered in faded red plastic along one side, then the counter, and finally the kitchen could be seen through a square window with a large flat shelf. Faded green swinging doors completed that side of the room. On the other side, beneath a large picture window, was a series of booths, also covered in the faded red plastic. In the far booth sat Fox, pretty and young; obviously the owner of the sports car outside, Coyote thought, and just as obviously as out of place in this place as a three dollar bill.

He ambled to the counter about mid-way down and sat on a slightly tipping stool. The swinging doors opened and Goose came in. She had a mound of hair piled on top of her head and wore a greasy apron that had once been some shade of green. Her mouth moved rhythmically with the chewing of a large wad of something.

"Whaddalitbe?"

"What have you got?" asked Coyote.

Goose looked at him with grey eyes, cold as polar ice caps.

"Do you have a menu?" asked Coyote. He thought to himself, 'I might have been asking her for her phone number, the way she's acting.'

After a moment of intense stare, Goose swung around, grabbed a greasy one sheet menu encased in a yellow transparent plastic and slapped it down in front of Coyote, swung around again with a swish of hips and was gone through the swinging door.

Coyote had just turned the menu right-side-up when Bear came through the swinging green doors. He was big, wearing an impossibly greasy T-shirt that just might have been white at some time. He walked up to the counter and leaned over Coyote. "You givin' Goosey trouble?"

"Mmem ... me?" stuttered Coyote. "No, sir! Not me. Just wanted something to eat and some coffee; been travelin' all day."

Bear closed his right eye and gave Coyote the once over. "Ok. That's what w'ere here for. But, no trouble, ya understand! I'll admit, this time a day Goosey ain't her best."

He no sooner disappeared through the green doors than Goose reappeared. "Whaddalitbe?"

This time, Coyote replied, "Coffee ... scrambled eggs with bacon and sourdough toast ... if you've got it." He still hadn't looked at the menu and decided not to.

"We got it; you got it." Goose scrawled something on a greasy green pad, tore the page off and stuck it on a spike in the window to the kitchen and yelled, "Order!" In seemingly a single motion, she turned, grabbed a cup from a shelf in one hand, the coffee pot off a burner in the other, and placed cup, filled with coffee in front of Coyote with a bored ease that bespoke years of practice. "Cream, sugar, on the counter."

With that, she plopped herself on a stool hidden behind the counter, picked up a ragged magazine, and began to read. The magazine had a scantily clad female on the cover and shouted something about 'Sex' so he figured it must be some sort of woman's magazine.

When he glanced at the spike, the ticket was gone.

With raised eyebrows, he sipped his coffee. It was hot and flavorless. Coyote revolved his stool about and looked out the window, seeing Fox out of the corner of his eye. Her eyes met his and she smiled. She had obviously been following the interplay with Goose and Bear. Behind Fox was a second window, smaller and shaded with some sort of blind that had small chunks missing from it.

Coyote grinned back, then gave her his put-upon look, and shrugged. Then he lost himself in the darkness beyond the window.

as told to Doug Hodges

A growl and a slam brought him back to the diner; Coyote figured his breakfast was ready. As he revolved back to the counter, he noticed that Fox had gone. Funny, he hadn't seen or heard her leave. He'd have to stop daydreaming like that.

Goose slid a plate in front of him, piled high with egg, bacon and toast. "Jelly, catsup, whatever, on the counter." Then, she was back to her stool and magazine. Coyote was about to ask for a coffee refill when he noticed it had been. 'They're efficient, I'll give them that.' He thought to himself.

While he was mulling over his coffee cup, letting the breakfast settle, the checked appeared as if by magic. Goose was still seemingly lost in her magazine.

Placing money on the counter, with a decent tip, Coyote said, "I'm sorry if I upset you earlier. The meal was good."

Goose looked up at him, so surprised she stopped chewing. Then, with a muttered "Da nada." She was back behind the lurid cover.

Coyote walked out. As he closed the door, he could see Bear's huge head peeping out the window from the kitchen.

He walked to the truck shaking his head.

His right front tire was flat.

He jacked up the truck, replaced the flat with his spare, and threw the flattened hunk of rubber in the bed. He neither saw nor heard any sign from inside the diner, not even a face at the window. He mounted up and drove off into the false dawn of the high plains.

Coyote was thinking, 'How appropriate.'

July, 1998

The Voice of Coyote

Raven and the Soul

Raven is a scavenger of souls.

One day he happened a young man, although all men are young to Raven, who had died by being literally torn apart. While Raven was pecking around the various limbs scattered here and there, looking for the soul, the man's head said, "I'm not ready to go. Please help put me back together and let me live. I'll bring you a thousand, no a million souls ... all at one time."

Now raven was not put off by a gamble but he was shocked. Death of such magnitude had always struck him as being unnatural, at the very least a product of overzealousness on someone's part.

He asked the head, "And, how would you do this?"

The head replied, "I am a great orator, a shaper and leader of men and times. I enflame passions ... love, hate, prejudice ... I've swayed the unwashed masses; I read humanity like a stock report; I can create wars ... genocide." Bodiless, the head lay on its side, looking eagerly at Raven, eyes large, bright and intense. the mouth drooled with anticipation, the head's tongue caressed its lips with a frenzy.

Raven said, "And, you would do this for me, just so you could live a little longer?"

"For myself, also." the head cried out, "And, for the world; for destiny. I don't belong like this here and now."

Raven shook his black plumage and plunged its beak deep into the head's neck, yanking out a squirming soul. Then, he flew up and down into the underworld where, he thought, such a soul truly belonged.

August 6, 1998

as told to Doug Hodges

Coyote and The Tooth

Coyote was having a problem with a tooth. A left incisor had split and a piece of meat was stuck there and was bugging him. It didn't hurt but it was an annoyance. And, the more Coyote thought about it, the bigger an annoyance it became.

Finally, he sought out a sandpiper. The little bird had a long narrow beak that Coyote thought would solve his problem.

"What shall you pay me?" said the bird.

"I won't eat you." replied Coyote.

That sounded good enough to the sandpiper and it probed around in Coyote's mouth with its long bill. But, try as it could, it couldn't jerk the piece of meat loose.

"I'm sorry, Coyote, but the meat's stuck too tight." said the sandpiper.

"Oh, all right." said Coyote. 'Maybe a jar will loosen it.' he thought.

So, Coyote banged his head on a large boulder. However, this only gave him a headache. 'OK,' thought he, 'something more drastic.'

Coyote found Bear. "Hit me in the jaw." he said.

"Whaa?" said Bear.

"Hit me in the jaw. I have some meat stuck in a tooth and need to have it knocked loose." explained Coyote.

"Whatever you say, old friend." Responded Bear as he swung one of his great paws in a roundhouse punch which knocked Coyote flying.

"How was that?" asked Bear.

Coyote picked himself up, felt the inside of his mouth with his tongue. "I think every tooth but that one is loose."

"Again?" asked Bear.

"No ... no, thanks ... I think I'll have to try something else." Muttered Coyote.

"Just a little." said Coyote, later that day as he watched the explosive being poured out onto a small piece of paper.

"Are you sure this is what you want?" asked the miner. "This stuff's pretty powerful."

"Quite sure." responded Coyote.

The Voice of Coyote

He took the explosive and ran up into the hills, packed the explosive around the tooth, forming a fuse, which dangled down from his mouth. Coyote then found a match and lit the fuse.

The ensuing explosion did solve Coyote's problem. It blew the meat out of the tooth; blew the tooth and all the rest of his teeth into pieces. As a matter of fact, the explosion blew Coyote's whole head to pieces.

However, of course Coyote can't die, so despite the mess, Coyote felt much better and the meat *was* gone.

September 29, 1998
given in the dentist chair

as told to Doug Hodges

A Death Of Coyote

Coyote was old, so gray with age that his fur was virtually white and so thin that the southwestern sun burned his skin. One day he decided he needed to figure out a way to beat this rapidly approaching death.

Now, Coyote knew he doesn't die and that he could appear in any shape or age he chose but such simplicity was not in his make-up. Nor even would the thought cross his mind, not when he could connive, plot and trick.

So, he thought and thought and decided he would be straight forward and ask someone to exchange time with him. Surely, there would be someone out there who had no use for time and was more than ready to leave this plain.

He went to various animal beings, all much younger than himself; his story always began, "Brother (or Sister) Bear (or Rabbit, Road Runner, Deer, Eagle, and so forth), there's so much I still have to do in this world. I have a family to watch over; I have great literature to write, great songs to sing. Would you trade your time with me?"

And, every time, they would reply, "Brother Coyote, I'm sorry, but I also have a family and too many things to do in this life."

Until one day, Coyote approached a young Raven with his plea. Now Raven, unlike the others, thought. 'A good sign.' thought Coyote.

Finally, Raven said, "I'll trade you time, Brother Coyote. But, you must do one favor for me."

"Ah!" murmured Coyote to himself, "At last. But, I must be careful. Raven has been known to be tricky."

"There is a black trail that Man uses ..." began Raven.

Coyote interrupted, "I don't much like dealing with Man."

"Nevertheless," continued Raven, "on the far side of this black trail is a pretty blue flower growing out of a cactus tree. I need you to pick it for me."

And why," asked Coyote, "can't you just fly over there and pick it yourself?"

"Because," spoke Raven, "it is a magic flower and I can only use it if the flower is given to me."

The Voice of Coyote

'Magic.' Coyote thought with a frown. 'This is not looking any better. Still, it is a chance to beat death and the task doesn't appear to be too difficult. And, a bargain is a bargain.'

"Ok, Brother Raven, you've got a deal."

Now, the world of Man, the world of Animal, and the world of Spirit, all exist together and separately. It is only the very wise, the very spiritual, or the very foolish that choose to interact between the worlds.

Man races huge, foul-smelling, beasts along his black trails, apparently without reason and definitely without care. An unholy graveyard of animal remains border these trails keeping the carrion eaters busy, and at risk, themselves; and Raven forever gathering souls.

However, Coyote thought, 'I can cross at night when the beasts can't see as well. Unlike animals Man and his creations have terrible night vision.'

With the last light of dusk, Coyote could see the blue flower, shining prettily and incongruously among the spines of the cactus tree.

He had waited until a moonless sky made the blackest night. Coyote, tensing his aging muscles, breathing in and out, deeply and slowly. The time had come. Coyote raced out across the black trail.

Light, brighter than a full moon, loomed up out of the darkness, freezing Coyote in his tracks. He was hit, split apart, and splattered across the black trail.

"Ouch!" thought Raven. "Poor Coyote. I'll have to remind him of this the next time he's feeling tricky."

Some time later, Coyote thought to himself, 'I should have known better.'

Texas
November 25, 1998

as told to Doug Hodges

Coyote Visits Rabbit and Raven

i

    Coyote's path, one day, led him to the very tall tree, which was the home of Rabbit and Raven. An elaborate R & R was carved into the tree about a third of the way up. Coyote thought it could stand for Rabbit and Raven but knew it really stood for Raven and Rabbit.

    When he threw his head way back and twisted his neck Coyote could see the balcony from which Raven generally entered and exited. Entrance was through an exquisitely arched opening, which was usually covered with thick dark velvet curtains.

    Whereas, in front of him was a not so ornate wooden door bearing a single round window. He watched Rabbit's face see him through the window, light up and smile. The door opened.

    "Coyote!" she cried, "What a pleasant surprise.!"

    "Just happened to be ..." he started.

    "I know," she interrupted, "'passing through'. It's good to see you. Come sit down. She took his hand and led him to the sofa. As he moved across the room, his gaze wandered, as always, to the photograph's of the ancient Raven family which were predominant on the wall, past Raven's trophies for this and that, to the spiral staircase that led up into a seemingly darkened forever. Coyote thought, as he always did, that the house was notable for it's lack of anything saying, "Rabbit."

    Rabbit swung him around and kissed him, desperately, hungrily.

    "I've missed you, traveler." she said.

    "I've missed you, too, Rabbit." he replied. "And, where is Raven this fine morning?" he asked.

    "Oh, he's at the usual 'morning' meeting of the Raven Roadkill Association. You know how those go. By the time, they've politicked everything and actually got out to the road, dined and then rehashed over everything they saw and ate, it's an all day affair."

    She pulled him down onto the sofa on top of her and they coupled.

    Afterwards, Coyote lay on the sofa admiring Rabbit as she moved about the room doing things he thought pointless and domestic.

The Voice of Coyote

"So," he asked, "will you ever leave him?"

"Raven?" she exclaimed, "Me? Of course not. You know that, Coyote. Raven and I are mates. We're happy."

"So, why do we make love?" he asked.

"We don't make love; we have sex." Rabbit said. "Raven's always so busy, so preoccupied with himself, it's just not satisfying. That's where you come in, O Roamer of the Land; you scratch my itch."

Coyote thought a moment and said, "I am honored. I do love you, though."

Rabbit looked at him and said, "I really do believe that. You love me when you're with me. I think you likewise love whomever you're with at the time. You live in the 'now,' Coyote. There's no past or future for you. And, that's fine for you. But, Raven and I are going to have children. He comes from a long and revered line. His children will soar through the skies of tomorrow."

Coyote thought how strange women could be, passionately businesslike, dispassionately attached. He sighed, got up, walked to her and began to nuzzle her neck.

ii

Later, they heard Raven arrive at the upper entrance. He came down the spiral stairs like a black-cloaked king, so shiny a black that traces of blue flickered within his coat.

"Ah, Coyote!" Raven exclaimed. "Here, again the world traveler. And, where have you been this time, my friend?"

"Here and there." Murmured Coyote. "Mostly there."

"Hah!" laughed Raven. "When are you going to settle down, get a wife, a job and become a productive member of society?"

'When Hell freezes over.' Thought Coyote. He said, "Everything in it's own time."

Raven just shook his head, and throwing his arm around Coyote's shoulder, led him across the room to a wide mantle over a cavernous fireplace, "Let me show you my newest bowling trophy. It's really something. But, the way I got it ... now, that was really a story."

"Rabbit, honey," said Raven, "Makes us some coffee, will you?" But, it was not a question.

"Sure." Said Rabbit and she was gone.

as told to Doug Hodges

"It started," Raven continued, "with a gentleman's bet, last summer, while I was bowling in the Willard International. You see …"

iii

Raven and Coyote had been friends all their lives. They both had intelligence, were sharp as a tack, and enjoyed life. But, where Coyote tried anything and everything, it was for the experience (all too often, for the fun) of it. Raven took everything deadly serious. Coyote and Raven played sports; Coyote never made the team, Raven was always the star. They did Scouts and public service together. Coyote survived, was well liked and was unmemorable; Raven wound up a hero, in the newspapers, and was the prize catch for all the young ladies. Raven was the darling of all the parents and leaders; Coyote was a nice guy. Raven would always be remembered; Coyote, who?

The key to their dissimilarities was that intensity and drive. Raven looked towards the future, using the past as a stepping stone. To him, Coyote had always been a gauge, a friendly rival, for Raven had (secretly) admired Coyote's gentleness, his easy-going personality, his apparent lack of a sense of responsibility. Coyote, as Rabbit had put so well, lived for the moment. Coyote gave his absolute best to things (in his own way) and was his own gauge and rival. He rarely thought about the past and so rarely learned from it. Yet, every moment was new to him, alive with magic and excitement. Coyote was too caught up in that moment to think about any future let alone a past that had come and gone.

Still, they had remained friends. Coyote visited Raven whenever in the area. The visit was all that more pleasurable when Raven mated with Rabbit for Coyote had always enjoyed Rabbit's company.

When Rabbit had turned him into an itch scratcher, Coyote didn't know what to think so he tried not to. Each time was a unique amazement to him, filled with pleasure, wonder, guilt and sorrow, in varying degrees.

At first he thought it would affect his relationship with Raven but he came to realize that any relationship that they had was only in Raven's world. Raven created his world from within and without. Things that didn't fit his perspective just didn't exist for him. Raven said the right things at the right time and had a patter that swayed the

The Voice of Coyote

masses. He was sensitive, compelling, and (Coyote thought) more often than not full of crap.

Sometimes, Coyote wondered if it would even make a difference if Raven knew what was happening between he and Rabbit (Hell, maybe Raven did). As long as it didn't affect his image, as long as it didn't threaten Raven's relationship with Rabbit, as long as Raven didn't have to acknowledge it …

Being an idealist and a Libra by nature, it was all too much for Coyote.

Yet, being Coyote, he still came visiting.

again from the dentist chair and beyond ...
December 15, 1998

as told to Doug Hodges

Grandfather Buffalo's Lesson

The winter came late bringing the snow down from the high mountains, into the foothills, and onto the high plains. It blanketed the hills and valleys in white and decorated the tree branches with jewels of ice.

Grandfather Buffalo was old, so old he dare not lay down for fear of not being able to rise. His beard and mane was white and thin. Still, he could move as fast as he needed, his horns thick and sharp. He was respected by all.

This morning, the young animals gathered around him, Deer, Elk, Rabbit and Buffalo. He was giving his annual winter talk. "Remember to stay together. There is safety and strength in numbers. It is the lean season for all, but especially hard on the meat-eaters; Hawk and Eagle, Cougar, Coyote and," he shuttered, "Wolf."

"They will risk much more to feed their families than in summer. It is imperative that you all remain together as you forage. Numbers provide strength and confusion."

"What of Raven?" spoke up one young Deer with just a trace of horn. "He is our friend and warns us of danger's approach."

Grandfather Buffalo looked at the young Deer with tired eyes. "He is our friend. But, he, too, will come for you, after you are dead and the slayer has gone."

He knew that some of the young ones would not heed his words and knew, also, that they would not live through the winter. But, that was the way of things. They would feed the families of the meat-eaters so that they, too, could survive.

Not too many days later, Grandfather Buffalo was grazing with a small herd through a field where they had beaten down the snow. He heard something in his head and looked up. Raven circled slowly overhead and then flew off to the north over a stand of aspen. Grandfather Buffalo started to follow.

"Where are you going, Grandfather Buffalo?" asked a young female Buffalo.

"Where I must." He replied. "It is my time."

"But ..." she started.

"It's all right." He said. "Stay here with the others."

The Voice of Coyote

He followed Raven's path through the stand of aspen, over a hill of fir and pine, and looked down into a small meadow. There, in knee-deep snow, a young Deer (the one who had questioned him earlier) was surrounded buy a pack of Wolves. Seven was their number.

The Wolves seemed in no hurry and just stood encircling the scared buck. A large grey, with one chewed-up ear, appeared to be the leader. He was evidently weighing pros and cons as to how to attack.

Grandfather Buffalo stately walked down the hill and into the circle forcing one female Wolf with three legs to scamper aside. She moved next to another Wolf and sat down, leaving the circle with an opening.

"I am here." said Grandfather Buffalo, to no one and everyone.

"Grandfather ..." began the young Deer.

"Go!" said Grandfather Buffalo, "Out the way I came."

"But," the Deer started to argue.

"Go! It is my time, now, not yours." intoned grandfather Buffalo.

And, the Deer was gone, quick as lightening through the break in the circle.

The three-legged female closed the circle by returning to her place.

"You honor us, Grandfather Buffalo." said the Wolf leader.

"And you me." Grandfather Buffalo replied. "You know I'll take one or more of you on my journey?"

"We know." The Wolf leader said. "It is the way of things."

Raven watched the unfolding tableau from a high branch up on the hillside.

He, too, felt honored. It was the way of things.

from Raven
December 24, 1998
Colorado

as told to Doug Hodges

Coyote In The Night

One day a group of animal elders were gathered. They were discussing the slaughter of their people along the black trail of man.

"So many have died." said Grandfather Rabbit from one side of the circle.

"That's true." said Grandfather Skunk from another.

Grandfather Porcupine nodded his head.

"But what can we do?" asked Grandfather Deer. "It lies across our path. At night, it can't even be seen." He arose and turned around inside the circle as he spoke. "The speeding light comes out of nowhere. It captures the eye and freezes my people in their tracks."

Coyote arose, "If I may speak, honored Grandfathers?"

Grandfather Deer returned to his place in the circle, looked around at the others, nodded to Coyote, saying, "Speak!"

"Times are bad." began Coyote. "The black trails have increased. They cross our lands like cracks in a dry river bed. Raven constantly complains at all the time he has to take with the dead. We don't count distance in lengths of space anymore, we count it in the bodies of our people."

"But," he paused and looked around, "I have a plan."

At this, not a sound was uttered. Yet, inwardly a great groan arose from all present, including Raven who was listening in a nearby cactus tree. All knew of Coyote's plans. Yet, Coyote was Coyote and one could not discount his magic, his age, his very spirituality. So all listened with some misgiving yet also with some hope.

"I," Coyote continued, "will study the black trail and watch the creatures of man. I will relay when the path across is clear to Road Runner, the swiftest of birds, who in turn will relay the message to the birds of the air, who in turn will relay the all-clear message to the animals wishing to cross. They will cross one at a time; each, only with an all-clear. Like any endeavor, success depends on stealth, speed, and silence."

"The Deer are the largest and fleetest. We should try the plan with them first. It if works for them, we will adapt it on down to the smaller and slower animals."

"Also," Coyote continued, "we must first try this at night, when the creature's wits are not at its best. We all know that Man is an animal of the day; so, it follows, will be his creation.

For weeks, Coyote lay in the shade of Sotal or Candelaria or Sequaro and watched and studied the black trail of Man and the strange creature that inhabited it; that flew by like the wind and came in various shapes and colors and stank like the foulest pool of stagnant water.

Finally, on the night of a Blue Moon, Coyote was ready. He gathered the elders of the desert and gave them the assignments for their people.

Coyote watched and gauged time and distance. The night was bright with the moon. Only the black trail, itself, seemed invisible as it seemingly melted into the desert to either side. But, there was no sign of man-life. There had not been such a sign on this trail at this time of night on all the nights Coyote had watched.

It was time. A small group of deer stood ready to cross about a mile south of him. The animal elders were all present, interest and perhaps a glimmer of hope in their eyes. Coyote whispered the signal that the path was clear. Road Runner picked up the message and ran to a flock of birds in a group of cacti on a hill; silhouettes in the moonlight looking like the dreaded man, themselves. These birds, in turn, flew into the night to the group of Deer.

Unfortunately, Deer are easily spooked, especially at night when all is shadow and vague. Even expected, the birds flying out of the night became shapeless and eerie-sounding shadows and spooked the Deer. They all ran pell-mell across the black trail, at the same time.

Immediately, almost as if cued, lights flashed from down the black trail. In less time than it took to register, they had grown brighter than the moon, and expanded out until it seemed that they targeted all living things, animal and bird, Coyote included. All were mesmerized, breath frozen, eyes widened.

With a roar like a desperate wind, a brief screeching and a thump, the lights shook, then continued their way down the trail until they disappeared like the light of a firefly.

One young doe had died and had been thrown across the trail.

"Well," said Raven, the only one with nerve enough to face Coyote in time of stress. "She got across."

as told to Doug Hodges

Coyote looked at him in disgust. Shook his head. "I'll never understand Man and his creature. They're not …" he searched for a word, "natural."

"They have no honor, no sense of responsibility, no … no understanding. They …" Raven stuck a black wing in Coyote's mouth.

"Hush, friend Coyote." Spoke Raven. "It's been a trying night. But, in all, one like many others. Man is apart and nothing that any of us can do will make him one of us. Because, simply, he's not."

"But …" started Coyote.

"Coyote!" Raven stopped him. "It's beyond us and, more importantly, is not really our affair. If we are to die, what matter if it's by Man's bullet or his beast of the black trail? For that matter, it more likely will be a fellow animal; some predator that will end this part of the journey. Or it could be a flood, a drought, a rock fall. It's not all that important, Coyote."

"But the elders depended on me." Coyote replied.

"Only because you gave them false hope." said Raven. "Admit that circle of life is beyond anyone's control, including your own. They will accept that."

The morning mist clung to the ground like a second skin, pale and opaque, as the council of elders dispersed. Coyote shook the sorrow from his mind and trotted off into the day. Raven smiled from a hidden perch and began to sing.

West Texas
January 27, 1999

Coyote Sings

Now, Coyote can sing. He sings 'in' the morning, creation, power, and life. However, like everyone else, Coyote also just sings when the mood takes him: in the shower, when in love, while drinking. He would probably sing while working but Coyote never thought of himself as working. At times, Coyote's singing would annoy his friends; fellows a lot less tolerant of the foibles of others than was Coyote.

Such a time happened one evening when Coyote, Eagle, Bear, Raven and Javalina (a name 'Pig' much preferred) were in a West Texas tavern consuming the local brew. Coyote was feeling pretty good and started to sing. He sang in a western drawl and was singing a not particularly soothing song of violence, death, and the glory therein. Though appropriate, given the present location and company, the song was not appreciated by Coyote's fellow imbibers. Javalina found the song particularly offensive as it talked about slaughter. Bear was upset because he, himself, couldn't carry a tune in a bucket and was glared at by the surrounding patrons whenever he tried to growl along. If he couldn't sing, he reasoned, Coyote shouldn't be allowed to, either. Eagle thought the song pointless and depressing. Raven was miffed because Coyote kept changing the words.

So, when Coyote left to find a tree or bush, the others put their heads together. Javalina spoke up, "We need to do something about Coyote's singing!"

"And what do you propose?" asked Raven.

"I don't know ..." replied Javalina. "but, something!"

"I can hit 'em." Bear said gleefully.

"I don't think that's the solution we're looking for, friend Bear." said Raven, "But, thanks for offering."

Eagle said, "We could just demand that he shut up. And, threaten to walk out on him if he doesn't."

"And, would you?" asked Raven, "Walk out?"

"Uh ... No. I wouldn't." Eagle shook his head. "I have as much right to be here as does Coyote."

"Of course, you do, friend Eagle." said Raven, "We all do."

Javalina cried out, "We can just have him thrown out!"

as told to Doug Hodges

"On what pretense?" asked Raven. "Apparently no one else is bothered. Otherwise he, and probably all of us, would already be out."

"Well, Mr. Know-it-all Raven," said Javalina, "what would you do to shut him up?"

"I?" replied Raven, "I would do nothing. It is a minor annoyance. If I were spiteful, I could do something back to Coyote that annoys him. Unfortunately, nothing seems to annoy him." Raven looked around and smiled, "Perhaps that's why he's our friend."

At that moment Coyote returned, ordered another round for their table, and broke into a Western Desert version of Greensleeves. His companions groaned audibly, yet each settled back into their own enjoyment of the time and place.

Javalina thought, "Well, at least he changed songs."

from the courtroom
February, 1999 - Colorado

The Voice of Coyote

Coyote and the Wind

Coyote roamed the Great Rift one day and he was bored. He strode to the top of a lava outcrop and shouted, "Oh, Spirit of the Wind, I am bored. There is no one to play with. Will you play with me?"

Now the Wind Spirit felt that he was much too important to be playing with that trickster Coyote. In fact, he felt offended that Coyote would even ask such a thing. Some of us have got better things to do with our time, he thought. I must teach Coyote a lesson.

So the Spirit replied, "Of course, Brother Coyote, I'll be happy too. However, I've been very busy of late. And, if we're to play, I need you to do one little thing for me first."

"And, what would that be, my Spirit Brother?" asked Coyote.

"I need you to carry some wind for me across the high plains and down into the desert." said the Spirit.

Coyote thought and said, "Can I do that?"

"Certainly!" said the Wind Spirit. "I'll tell you how."

"Take three deep breaths and let each out very slowly. This will relax and prepare you body. Good! Now exhale all of your breath until you feel yourself as thin and helpless as a weed. Now, slowly, inhale ... and keep on inhaling. I'll help you. That's the way."

And Coyote inhaled and inhaled until it seemed his very seams would burst. Still more air came in and even more.

Finally, when he thought he was well beyond the bursting stage, the Wind Spirit said, "Fine! That's fine. You can stop now. I believe you have enough. I was only going to send a small wind, anyway. Now, on your way, Friend Coyote. I'll wait here for your return. Oh, by the way, did I tell you? You must not let the wind go. No, sir! Under no circumstances. Otherwise, it will follow you ... forever ... wherever you go. Goodbye."

As Coyote ran away, as fast as his inflated bulk would allow, he thought he heard the Wind Spirit laughing. He began to think maybe he'd been had.

But, it was too late to do anything else; so on he ran and ran, the wind trying to escape with every jolt of foot to the ground.

The farther he went, the more insistent the wind seemed to become. It wanted to leak out of Coyote's jaws, his nostrils, his ears,

as told to Doug Hodges

and ... well, anyplace it could escape. Coyote concentrated on keeping it in. He concentrated so hard on this that, somewhere along the Pecos, he tripped and fell.

Rolling over and over he tried so hard to keep in the wind it hurt. He had just stopped rolling and was starting to mentally congratulate himself on the incredible save when Raven came zooming out of the sky.

Raven had been lonely and was looking for someone to play with. Coyote would never have been his first choice but he was the only game in sight so Raven decided it was time for some Raven tag. This is a game in which Raven attacks and badgers some four-footed creature, Wolf was the most fun, until the beast is dancing on its hind legs, snapping at the air, whirling itself in frenzied circles ... it was Raven's favorite game.

Coyote just had enough time to think, 'Oh, no!' when Raven plowed into his stomach. The wind came out with a huge whooosshh blowing Raven back into the air and imbedding Coyote inches into the soil. The wind circled round and round over Coyote as if happy to be free.

"What's all this?" shouted Raven, peering down through the swirling dust. "You are so strange, Coyote. I never know what to expect from you." and with a disgusted "Kwaawk," Raven flew off without waiting for an answer.

Just as well, thought Coyote. He wouldn't have like any answer I would have given him.

Coyote got up, dusted himself off. The wind flew over and around him. He started walking back the way he had come. The wind dipped and danced and would flitter here and there, caressing rocks and trees, following Coyote.

from West Texas ... Kansas ... Wyoming ... Colorado ...
wherever Coyote roams
March 29, 1999 - Southern Colorado and the Blue Moon

Storm

Grandfather Buffalo was alone. Alone on a prairie of thigh-deep grass as far as he could see in all directions.

The grass moved, in rippling waves, with the August wind; blowing cool from the unseen mountains to the west.

Grandfather Buffalo knew Brother Wolf could be there, stalking in the tall grass. Or even The People, moving quietly on all fours like the very prey they hunted.

Yet, he was not concerned. What would be, would. Without any thought on his part.

The sky, which but a moment before had been a bright blue and cloudless, now filled with rolling white, rippling like the grass, he thought. Streaks of blue between bands of white, were shrinking until all was swirling white. In the distant west, the clouds were dark and seemingly rolled on top of the horizon.

A storm was coming.

Grandfather Buffalo was glad that he was old and no longer a part of the herd. He had reached the stage where he could no longer keep up and, so, was left behind. It was the way of things.

A storm would create unease, if not outright panic, within the herd. As the eldest, all would look to him for guidance, for assurance, for safety. And, as always, the herd would weather the storm. But, there would be losses; the very young, the very old, the very unlucky. The last death being just as weighty as the very first.

These were ever hard to take upon his shoulders, no matter how broad.

Now, he would face the storm alone. Oddly, for a herd creature, the thought did not bother him.

He faced into the wind, which blew his beard and mane. The coolness felt good, yet there was a chill beneath that he sensed more than felt. The sky above grew ominous; dark rolling waves. Lightning flashed and the sound of a stampede came to his ears. A stampede, he knew, not made up of legs and flesh and bone.

The rain came with the wind, beating at the grass, mowing it like a scythe.

Grandfather Buffalo stood, like a boulder on the plain, unmovable.

as told to Doug Hodges

Then, as sudden as it had come, the storm was passed.

A new sound came. Like distant thunder but different.

Previously unseen gullies, now filled with rushing water, became riotous rivers, sweeping along everything encountered as they ate their way across the plain. Trees, errant wildlife, rock and earth ... all was swept along even as the sky above cleared and the sun began to dry Grandfather Buffalo's coat. But, he could hear the torrent rage; the crying of the earth as it moved and changed.

He stood upon an edge, the grass darkened by the rain. The gully below him roared and he felt the earth tremble beneath his hooves.

Brother Horse went by, apparently dead; just another muddy swirl in the tempest water. Then, its rider ... Brother Man vainly trying to keep his head above the constantly changing surface. Arms flailing, thrashing, a silent tableau in the shriek of the storm's aftermath.

It was not one of The People as it wore a strange shiny coat. This puzzled Grandfather Buffalo for only a moment. The world was ever changing.

Then, it was quiet. As if the Earth Spirit had taken its final breath. Quiet and over.

The transition from overwhelming noise to complete lack of sound seemed almost unnoticeable to the ear. The sun shone bright and hot in the baby-blue fullness of the sky. The earth, just moments previous saturated with water, was already beginning to dry, the grass raising itself upright.

Grandfather Buffalo looked at his feet and the gully below, already empty of water. His perch had held.

It was not yet his time.

He was amazed and gave thanks to the Spirits of Wind and Rain, to the Great Spirit for this strange, unfathomable path upon which he roamed.

Turning around to the sparkling expanse before him, Grandfather Buffalo shook his heavy head, slinging deeply embedded drops of water. Then, he bent down and began to munch on the tall grass waving gently in the breeze of the high plains.

from Buffalo
June 7-17, 1999
in the skies above the midwest and the east coast

The Voice of Coyote

The Dolphin and the Pelican

Time weighed heavy on Pelican's mind.

He was bored and his life seemed to lack purpose. He flew in formation with his friends and family, peeling off and swooping down to skim the water's surface; diving down upon sparkling unsuspecting fish ... to swallow, soar upward, to only reform again with his comrades against the puffy white clouds of the sky. It was all very well, thought Pelican, if you're mind was narrow, if you didn't want something more.

As endless and wonderful as the sky appeared, to Pelican, it had limitations. He always found himself having to settle on land. As mysterious and magical as the ocean was, Pelican could only briefly dive through it, not truly becoming a part of its existence ... like Dolphin.

He did envy Dolphin, whom he saw as endlessly playing among the waves. Two by two, male and female, they leapt and dived and flashed along the surface like silver waves, themselves. Oh, they ate and mated, and did all the things inimitable to life but they had such fun ... such unconcerned naturalness to their movements. Pelican just thought of the endless series of foraging, formations, and boredom that lay ahead of him. I will ask Dolphin, he thought, what I can do. They are wise and happy so must have all the answers.

"Brother Dolphin," asked Pelican one bright day, as he sat upon the jetty, "I want to be happy. I want to be able to play and be in harmony ... I want to have fun. What is your secret?"

Dolphin replied, "I have no secret. I just am. I fill each moment with all that I can, feeling all the sensation, all the emotion, absorbing and giving ... sharing all that I am. I move through this life-path of mine as much as I can, being one with all life, being in harmony as much as I can be."

"Yes ..." said Pelican. But, this answer did not satisfy him. "But, I am one with my environs, with my species. The sky is not as much fun as the sea. Searching for food is not fun. Following formations and rules is not fun. How do you live without such detriments to joy?"

"My dear Pelican," Said Dolphin. "There are no detriments to joy, other than those you, yourself, create. I and my mate are of the sea. It is our mother, our life, our connection to the world. Through her, we can do and be anything our bodies allow us. We, too, have challenges

as told to Doug Hodges

that test our mettle but life gives us what it will and we, in turn, do what we can and must and give what we have in return.

You, Pelican, are of the air, and land, and sea. You can do things and see places those of us tied to the sea can only dream of. Yes, we can do things and see places that you cannot. It is the way of our separateness. But neither of us is greater nor must be happier in our existence. For each of us has our own path. The threads of our individual paths is what makes up the whole of existence.

I am not wiser than you, but maybe a little more accepting and understanding. I can only say to you, 'Feel.' Do not think or fret or worry. Feel your path. Let the earth and sky and sea speak to you. Let the Spirits guide you.

Share this wisdom gained and as you are taught, you will also teach. Each of us is like a pebble thrown into a smooth mirror-like pond. Our existence ripples out as we affect the world about us. We encounter the ripples of others as they do ours."

Pelican thought and said, "Thank you, Brother Dolphin. You have given me much to think on."

He flew out across the gently lapping waves of the sea and up into the panorama of cloud and sky. His brother joined him. Then his two cousins … four became eight and a V-shaped formation was formed which swept against blue and white, growing smaller until it was lost in the distance.

Dolphin chuckled to himself. His mate called him by name and asked what was so funny. He replied, "I'll never understand why so many creatures strive so hard to be miserable. When happiness is always at the tip of paw or wing or fin. They just have to 'be.' I wonder why that is so hard for so many to see?"

"Because, Querida," replied his mate, "they think too much. They rely too much upon their own devices. They believe they, as individuals, are the world, not merely a piece of it. They don't see themselves as a thread in a tapestry or a puzzle piece in the whole picture. Until they do and can feel that connection, they will be ever lost, seeking a connection, a home, that they themselves have severed."

"It is so." Replied Dolphin with a sigh. He smiled and snorted water over her face. And, they were off in a chase through the waves, laughing and leaping.

from Pelican
Brownsville, TX, June 1999

The Voice of Coyote
A Lesson In Stuffing

Coyote was stuffed ... literally. He stood on a log in the front window of a 'Western' store in San Antonio, around the corner from the Alamo. He felt it quite an indignity.

The shop's owner was an old Texan with long dyed mustachios, long thinning hair swept back, who walked like he'd spent a lifetime in the saddle, which he had. He had bought Coyote a number of years ago from a young, apparently poor, Spanish speaking fellow who had come north out of the Rio Grande Valley. The animal had been recently killed, and as it was not politically incorrect in those days, the old cowboy looked at Coyote thinking that he might mount well, which he did.

So, Coyote watched the inner workings of downtown San Antone for a good number of years; saw buildings change, come and go; and the endless stream of people ... people, like rabbits, he thought.

One day, Coyote just got so disgusted at the noise and stink and hustle and bustle ... or maybe he just finally got bored ... that he decided to do something. He had been placed on the log in a downward position, head lower than the hind end, teeth barred, one foot on a protruding branch. So, he turned himself around, head high and more or less lounging, back against the log, hind feet on the branch. After running his tongue over his teeth, which by this time had seen better days, he grinned his old "Hey, I'm Coyote!" grin.

He made this movement slowly and deliberately while a number of people were looking in the window. One exclaimed, "Sure is interestin' how they make these critters move nowadays." Another replied, "Yeah, electronics can do anything. So lifelike."

The neighboring storeowner, whose name was Bob, and who sold T-shirts and Texas memorabilia in his 'Texas' store, and wouldn't know wildlife from a hole in the ground, walked into the 'Western' store about noon. "Tom! Wasn't that Coyote posed differently, before?"

Tom, the old cowboy, ambled out of the store and looked in the window. "Yep!" he said, and went back in.

"Well," said Bob, following at Tom's heels, "how'd you do that? You've had that moth-eaten thing in the window since I started up and that was, what, six years ago or more. Why change it now?" He

as told to Doug Hodges

then muttered more to himself; "It does look better in that position but still is pretty offensive."

"Never touched it, Bob." said Tom, always a man of few words. Bob thought that was one reason the 'Western' shop was full of a lot of stuff that didn't seem to sell. However, he couldn't get passed the fact that Tom, while never apparently selling anything, always kept his store full of people (no accountin' for taste) and was evidently prosperous. Tom was still there when many, too many, businesses had come and gone.

"Whaddaya mean, you never touched it? It's changed." Bob reiterated.

"I know." Replied Tom. "I just didn't change it."

"Then, who did?" enquired Bob.

"Coyote, I reckon." Said Tom, silently wishing that Bob would just go away.

"Whaddaya mean, Coyote?" asked Bob.

"I mean Coyote! What do you think I mean. He can do any dang thing he wants." And, with that, Tom stomped off into the back of his store, behind a dusty buffalo skin.

Bob just starred off after him. "Old coot!" he shouted. Definitely gone 'round the bend, he thought.

Interesting, though. He walked out of the store but couldn't get past Coyote in the window. The expression on the animal's face seemed to hold him, like some sort of trap. So different, almost mocking ... ridiculous, Bob thought. Yet ...

Well, Tom has had that thing forever and it gives the neighborhood a bad look. Best thing I could do for San Antonio, thought Bob, would be to buy it and burn it ... put it out of it's misery. It can't cost all that much.

"Tom!" he shouted as he re-entered the 'Western' shop.

Well, it did cost all that much; $35 bucks for an old, moth-eaten, stuffed animal with fur rubbed off and sticky with God knows what having been spilled on it over the years. That crazy cowboy had wanted $75. Bob had almost choked when he heard that. That old man oughta be locked away somewhere. Finally pleading, practically begging, Bob had gotten the old cowboy to come down in price. "Only because you're a fellow storekeeper ... sort of." Tom had said, looking him up and down, from the large white ten-gallon straw cowboy hat, passed the T-shirt with a glaring Texas flag on the back and the store's logo modestly displayed on the pocket in the front, to the designer jeans, and finally the shiny red boots apparently made out of some exotic critter's skin. Tom thought to himself, I sure bet that's not real leather.

"You don't believe in mounting critters, anyway. What you want ole Coyote for?" he had asked.

"Just to get it off public display." Bob had lightly said on his way out. But, to himself, he wondered just why had he bought the darned thing.

Oh, well, Bob thought, he had it now. He lounged in the back room of his 'Texas' shop. Sure doesn't fit in with the T-shirts and posters even if he had been the type of person to go along with taxidermy. As it was, he wasn't. He could think of nothing more disrespectful to a fellow creature to be killed, stuffed, and put on display in some silly position for all eternity, or at least until the carcass completely rotted.

He'd take it out back of his trailer and burn the thing in the incinerator when he got home … but it sure does seem to be looking at him. No matter what position Bob took in the room, Coyote's eyes seemed to be glued to him, watching him, like the darned thing was aware. An illusion, he thought, reflection from the fake eyes.

After a while, feeling a little uneasy, Bob put Coyote in a large white plastic bag bearing a great flag of Texas and modestly imprinted with the logo of his store. He forgot about Coyote, then, until he was closing up that evening and caught sight of the large bag with the corner of his eye. Almost as an afterthought, he snatched it up on his way out the door.

Now, Bob lived in a newer trailer park at the beginning of the hill country in the north end of the city. It was shiny and glitzy, with a gate at the entrance. Bob pressed in his secret code on the keypad, the gate opened, he drove through, waved at a neighbor he recognized but didn't know, and drove up to his place, a big double-wide rectangle, in silver and blue plastic, sitting on a concrete pad surrounded by a small lawn that the 'association' kept mowed.

As he drove around the semi-circle to his shiny double-wide, Bob passed by the big trash compactor/incinerator. He thought about maybe leaving the bag containing Coyote. No, upon second thought, he'd better dispose of it himself, late, when no one could see him.

as told to Doug Hodges

Bob got his mail out of the key-lock and walked to his trailer, Coyote under one arm. Once inside, he tossed Coyote nonchalantly in the corner next to the closet. Bowie, his gray French Poodle was running around and jumping up and down like always when he returned home. He patted the dog's head, gave him a treat from a sack on the counter and slid open the sliding glass door to let him into the fenced back yard. However, Bowie had sensed something different and was nosing the discarded white bag.

"Leave that alone, Bowie." Shouted Bob. "No telling what germs and disease that thing's carrying.

Finally, Bob got the dog out but Bowie came back in as quick as he could and returned to the bag containing coyote.

Bob sat down with a great sigh in his large easy chair opposite the 54" screen digital color TV and said, "C'mon Bowie." But, instead of jumping into Bob's lap like usual, Bowie would not leave the bag. He kept nosing and clawing at it.

"Well," said Bob, getting up with effort, "if ya got to see the darned thing, let me get it out for you."

He snatched the bag away from Bowie and pulled Coyote free. Pretty wretched-looking and disgusting he thought.

Bob carried Coyote over to the fireplace he had never used. A great set of imitation long horns hung on the wall. There was no mantle. He looked around and saw a small table bearing a stack of magazine he had been planning to dispose of, Sports Illustrated and Playboys mainly. He hated to get rid of them because you never knew when you wanted to refer back to one.

He set Coyote on the floor, took the magazines and set them on the floor under the table, and placed Coyote, after removing Bowie, who had sunk his teeth into one mangy haunch, back on top of the table.

Actually, he thought, stepping back, that fits pretty well. Doesn't even look too bad, if one was into that sort of thing.

So, Bob and Bowie and Coyote became a trio, of sorts.

Bowie grudgingly accepted Coyote after one evening when Coyote growled back and snapped at him. Bob never did get around to having Coyote destroyed. As a matter of fact the thought never even came to mind, even upon the rare occasion when Tom would ask him, "What'd you ever do with old Coyote?" He'd just reply blankly, "What Coyote?" And go about his business.

Coyote would sit on his log on the table and watch the world go by on Bob's 54" TV. Occasionally, he'd change position. Tom would tell himself, "Nah!" Bowie didn't care.

July-August 1999 - San Antonio, Texas

as told to Doug Hodges

Coyote and the Cowboy

Coyote looked around.

South Texas was warm, humid and pretty much flat. The flatter areas still held water from the late-departed hurricane. Here and there sand dunes gently rolled like white waves; elsewhere scrub brush and cactus trees dotted the landscape.

A Cowboy was rolling a cigarette, one leg hooked over the saddle horn. His pony, beneath him, appeared to be leaning against a fence post, asleep. There was no longer any fence attached to the post.

Coyote came upon them about the time the brain tablet was done and the cowboy held it between his lips. His left hand struck a Lucifer off a concho on his chaps and he lit up. The pony opened his eyes, without moving his body, and eyed Coyote suspiciously. One mangy cow could be seen off in the distance.

"Hola, vaquero!" greeted Coyote.

The cowboy studied Coyote from eyes hidden beneath the wide brim of his rainshed. "Howdy." he replied as he continued with his makings.

Coyote made a great effort of looking around him and asked the cowboy, "How many head do you run on this range?"

"Ah, Coyote." Replied the cowboy in a slow-drawling voice, his unseen eyes twinkling, "about 5000 head ... of cactus. Maybe a doggy or two."

"Had a bull once ..." The cowboy fumbled in his shirt pocket for another match, fired this one with his thumbnail, and re-lit his cigarette, which had gone out. After a long draw, he went on, "apparently lost it in the storm. Too heavy to move fast, I guess, and got washed away."

"You don't fool me, Senor." Said Coyote, coyly "Someone as important as you, out here with nothing to watch? I'm sure there must be many cattle ... perhaps scattered from the hurricane."

"Perhaps." The cowboy replied, amiably. "Don't rightly know. If'n I did, I don't think I'd be tellin' you, anyhow."

"Oh, come on!" said Coyote. "We're both creatures of the world. You know harmless old Coyote. What possible harm could I do to a herd of cows?"

The Voice of Coyote

"Well, I'm just a no-account waddie but I do know you can be pretty devious and downright sneaky at times." The cowboy gently kneed his horse which came to life, glanced at Coyote a last time, hummpffed, and began to slowly move off. The cowboy shoved the cigarette makings inside his shirt pocket, touched the brim of his hat with his right hand, and with nary a sound Coyote was staring at a broad red-checked back.

"Senor!" cried Coyote, hurrying to keep up with the quick walk of the cow pony. "I mean no harm. I'm just making conversation. It's a long lonely trek across the valley and I would like some companionship. Could I accompany you to wherever it is you are going?"

Horse and rider stopped.

"Sure! Just keep up with ole Bill." Said the Cowboy.

Ole Bill lifted a hind leg and hummpffed again.

"I'd offer you a ride but I don't think Bill would stand it."

"Don't concern yourself, Senor." Said Coyote. I was born to the land. My legs are still an umbilical cord."

With that, the three moved west, inland away from the sea.

Coyote appeared at times to lead. Uncannily, he seemed to know just when the cowboy would turn his pony and in what direction; he knew what clump of brush the waddie would check out, even before the cowboy did himself.

They continued in this manner through the morning and into the early afternoon finding no cows or much anything of any importance. Barely a word was said.

The cowboy stopped, dismounted, and unsaddled his pony. He looked at Coyote, who had sat down and started licking his right front paw, "We'll rest awhile here in the heat of the day, put on the nosebag and siesta. I'll be ridin' into the night to make the ranch house."

There was little said during the break. The cowboy seemed preoccupied with a mesquite stick; the pony appeared to be asleep on his feet; Coyote seemed to just stare off into the chaparral.

Finally the cowboy moved, packed his belongings, saddled and loaded his horse, then swung up into the kak.

"Coyote!" The cowboy looked down. He slid on a pair of tan leather gloves. "Normally, I know you're good at jawin' and a pleasant companion. I'd usually love your company."

as told to Doug Hodges

The cowboy scratched his chin and the two-day stubble. "But, somethin's funny today. I have the strongest feelin' that I just cain't trust you. Perhaps I know too much about you."

Coyote looked up and replied, "Senor, perhaps you know too little?"

"In any event," the cowboy said, "we'd best part ways, now. Adios, Coyote."

"Adios, caballero!" said Coyote. "Another day, perhaps?"

"Quien sabe!" And, cowboy and pony were off at a fast trot. The pony didn't even hummpff.

Coyote sat awhile and pondered until his left hind leg started scratching. Then, he scampered off, heading south to the Rio Grande.

August 27, 1999
– the millennium

Texas Wolf

Wolf was old, old and wise. He was not supposed to be in Texas, neither here on the plains nor anywhere else. Man denied his existence. That was all right with Wolf.

As a pup, Wolf had crossed the muddy Rio Bravo with his parents. The river had been good, a haven for game and the mud kept the hot sun from his skin.

Wolf's little cousin, Coyote, was everywhere. Wolf's father used to say that Coyote was worse than Rabbit at proliferation because he knew better.

But Wolf was glad for Coyote. Being the only prey of any sustenance, Coyote had kept Wolf alive in lean times.

Other than his parents, Wolf had not seen any of his kind since the great river crossing. His father died from a rancher's bullet; his mother died from a trap. She had bled to death after chewing her left hind leg off. Wolf was alone.

Working his way across the saltpans and sand dunes of the gulf area, Wolf meandered into the hill country, despite the overwhelming scent of man and cow, and briefly onto the desert of greenless mountains and endless variety of cacti. Eventually, his instinct for survival brought him to the northern plains of Texas. Here, there was game and water, shelter and, most of all, space in which to be lost, an abundance of space.

Along a lonely stretch of metal rails, Wolf came upon a deer that had died. The cause of death was not apparent but the carcass was fresh, whole, and smelled all right.

This was the metal road of man. It formed a slight hill that ran as far as the eye could see if both directions. Wolf knew little of it.

It was not the stinking trail of black, sticky death usually associated with man. Yet, was nonetheless of his making. It carried a creature that Wolf had only heard, whining in the night leaving its own stink.

The body of the deer lay across the two metal bands. As Wolf angled himself to see the best way to move the body his left hind leg got caught between the gravel and the metal rail.

as told to Doug Hodges

He thought to himself, all of his wisdom couldn't save him from his instinct, this nature to take food wherever it was found, not counting the risk. Now, he'd probably end up like his mother.

Try as he could, the leg could not be released.

He felt something. A pulse in the metal bar that began with a tingling and rapidly turned into a physical sound. He looked up.

A great light, no three lights, a three-eyed beast was roaring out of the night. It was all he could do not to wet himself. So, this is how it ends. Man wins again, he thought.

The movement and sound became one as the very earth began to shake. Closer and closer came the eyes. A high piercing scream came from the beast.

As the ground shook about him, Wolf continued to try to free his leg. Yes, it moved. Just a little. More now. Hurry, he thought. The creature is upon him.

And in a rush of sound and black cloud, blacker than the night, Wolf rolled away as a gigantic hand brushed him aside like he would a flea.

He lay panting, some distance away, watching a single red eye recede into the distant dark.

When he could walk, it took a while for his legs to stop shaking, what was left of the deer was just a soggy pulp. Anything recognizable had been taken along with the suction of the beast.

He decided then and there that there were worse things than starvation. He would never again allow himself to again be tempted and trapped by man. He chuckled. Rather, by his own self, he admitted.

Wolf trotted off, still hungry, still old, still wise, and still alive.

Texas Panhandle
September 15, 1999

Coyote and the Traveling Companion

One gorgeous day Coyote ambled south of the Rio Bravo in an area known as the Serranias del Burro. At a bend in the river he came upon a tiny village. There, at the edge of the water, was a human girl child playing. She had long brown hair which blew wild and free in the gentle breeze, dark depthless eyes and wore a simple white cotton dress which she dutifully folded and placed on a rock while she played in the muddy-looking water.

Obeying propriety as much as he usually did, Coyote waited until the girl was done playing and had dressed herself and was about to leave when he approached. "Hola, child, greetings of the day to you." He said.

The girl started, then looked Coyote up and down. She backed up two steps and replied, "Hola, yourself, Coyote. I don't speak to strangers. Goodbye!"

"Hold on a moment." begged Coyote. "I'm not a stranger. I am Coyote. You know me!"

"Si! Mama says you're the worse of all strangers."

"Aiee! Slander!" shouted Coyote.

Seeing the girl start to back off, he quieted his voice. "Listen, muchaca, por favor, I wouldn't hurt you. I'm a good guy. I just want to talk for a moment. I have a proposition for you."

The little girl's eyes went wide.

"No!" he cried ('definitely the wrong word,' he thought). "I mean I have something I'd like to ask you, something important. Couldn't you spare me just a moment?"

"I suppose … if you stay over there and don't come any closer … I can listen … for just una momento."

"Gracias, little one. I don't think you'll be disappointed."

Coyote posed himself, looking around and at the sky, pacing this way and that, then sat down, cocked an eye at the girl and began.

"I travel everywhere. I do many things. But I get lonely. I seek a companion to share my travels, my adventures. I see you here, all radiant and blooming like a desert wildflower. I say to myself, here's one who may like to better her life, who may want something more."

as told to Doug Hodges

"Something more than what?" asked the girl, who began brushing her hair with a wide-toothed comb she had removed from her pocket.

"Why," replied Coyote, "something more than growing up, getting married, having children like a rabbit, getting fat and wrinkled, and never living any further than this desolate hunk of land, this dirty river, the hot breeze."

He went on before she could say a word. "I can take you to high cool mountains, to large cities full of life and fantasy, to seas and skies beyond your imagination."

"Why don't you take Senora Coyote? I was told that you make her great with pups and then leave her when they are born."

"More tales! Besides, she is not much of a traveler. She has her own path ... and I, mine. I would share mine with you."

The girl stopped her brushing, pulled some hairs from the comb and put the green plastic back in her pocket. She looked Coyote straight in the eye and said, "If I were a half century in years and fat and wrinkled, would you still want me? If I had tasted of life, good and bad, would I still be desirable? Is it the fact that I am young, new ... a slate to be written upon ... by you perhaps ... is that why you want me?"

In his silence, the girl turned to walk away, and then, suddenly, faced Coyote again. "I would not like to be left on a cold and lonely mountain or in a city with its fearsome masses. Here, all are my friends and family. My path may appear simple but it is mine. I can change it when and how I choose. Perhaps it would be hard, but I would do it if I so chose and in my own time. Thank you very much, anyway, Senor Coyote." And with that, she was gone back up the trail to the tiny village.

Coyote thought and muttered under his breath. "Aiee, yes, I believe I would want you a half century old, fat and used, abused ... but so grown, I think. I do believe you will come out all right. You do not need me ('much less want me,' he thought).

He made himself a mental note to return in about 40 years. Then, deciding he had spent enough time, he crossed the river to a land where things were not so straightforward.

October 13, 1999
Old Hwy 802- Brownsville, Texas

Coyote On the Island Or Coyote and the Great Blue Heron

It was a gorgeous Texas sundown. Coyote watched from the bayside of the Island as the sun burned red into the placid and salty water of the bay. Behind him, a full moon arose over the warm surf of the living sea.

A wide variety of birds gathered on the beach, but one, in particular, caught Coyote's eye. It was a great Blue Heron, which stood apart from other birds out on a sand bar, patiently waiting for fish to swim by. It would bend itself over and with its long bill virtually spear down, skewering a fish, then deftly slide the fish down and off the spear-like bill to be caught in its mouth. So graceful and quick it was that Coyote was amazed and decided to get a closer look.

When the Heron didn't move, it was a black silhouette against the burning ball of sun. Coyote waded slowly, quietly upon the bird which stood upon a small sand bar. When he was mere yards away, Heron spoke, "Hello Coyote. Greetings of the evening to you."

"Hello Bird." Said Coyote. "Have you known long that I was here?"

"A while." Replied Heron. "I have sharp eyes."

Coyote said, "I have never seen a bird like you, before. Besides looking like some sort of gangly tree, you do have grace and astounding speed. Of course, I saw you indecisively moving this way and that like your head was cut off before you settled on a spot to wait."

"Did no one ever tell you, Coyote," replied Heron, "if you couldn't say something nice not to say anything at all?"

"No," said Coyote, "I believe I missed that one." He was looking down into the water. Heron was standing in about three inches of the sea. "How can you catch fish big enough for a meal in such shallows?" he asked.

"The level changes drastically moment to moment." Said Heron, "And besides, you'd be surprised just how little depth fish need to survive."

as told to Doug Hodges

"Is that so?" muttered Coyote.

A blue crab scuttled along beneath his gaze.

Coyote looked up at Heron. "Well, I am impressed by your nose."

Heron looked at Coyote. "I've heard your nose is pretty sharp, also."

With that, Coyote nodded and waded back to shore, glancing one last time at the black silhouette against the blood red ball now more than halfway melted into the black of the horizon.

South Padre Island, Texas – Fall, 1999

Coyote Along The Border

"Man is full of anger and frustration; his lot in life is to suffer, to do his best, to live and to die." Thus spoke the young Mexican warrior. His face was lost in the shadow of a wide-brimmed sombrero but his voice betrayed the fear and uncertainness of youth.

Coyote sat across the small fire from the boy; flames jerked and popped and the scent of mesquite drifted about them. It was a dark night. Sweat mingled with humidity. Invisible clouds hid the stars. There was no moon.

"Why do you fight?" Coyote quietly asked.

"Por que?" The boy thought a moment.

"Because it is what is. One can do nothing else in this time. The soldados steal and rape and kill ... the banditos steal and rape and kill. Homes are looted; fields are burnt and trampled by horses. It is a bad time. I would hate to be a woman in this time.

He paused, looked up. Coyote thought he saw fire in a pair of hidden eyes or maybe it was just a reflection of the flames. "It is a time of death and war. One must become war to survive."

"In times of growth and life ... then, one must become life, a farmer, a husband, a father of many children. But, that is not my time."

"Perhaps, it will be some day, compadre." Spoke Coyote. "We must all have hope."

"The ruales kill us. The banditos kill us. The Americanos kill us.

"All want to use us and take from us everything we have, including our lives.

"What else is there for us but to fight and pray Dios, for whomever, whatever, for a better day; any day being better than the present one.

"We are a passionate people, Senor Coyote. Our wars are bloody and violent. They may seem pointless to an outsider."

Coyote spoke, "All wars are pointless."

"But, they bring change!" exclaimed the soldier.

"They bring death." Said Coyote.

"Death is common," replied the youth, "and not to be feared."

"Life is common," said Coyote, "and not to be feared."

as told to Doug Hodges

"War is God's will." The youth was pacing now. "For the people to overthrow oppression."

Coyote scratched his shoulder. "God gives us a path. But, it is we who choose to walk that path or not ... and in what way."

"War is a cleansing ..." the man went on, "of the corrupt, of the evilly stagnant ... of the soul, itself."

"War," replied Coyote, "is death. Nothing more. Nothing less."

"You don't understand!" cried the man. "How could you? You are only an animal. What do you know of glory, of greatness, of movement? The names of Villa and Madero shall be on the tongues of man long after you are gone."

"Perhaps." Coyote asked, "And, will the world be a better place for that?"

Silence fell on the small dry wash where the two huddled about the tiny fire.

Coyote slowly shook his head. Even to him, the paths of life often seemed puzzling.

The soldado picked up his rifle and stared at it as if it were a snake. "The Rio Grande is a grand river, but it has been baptized in blood."

Said Coyote, "The earth is a grand earth but it has been baptized in blood."

"Must you parrot me?" cried the youth as his charged to his feet. He kicked out the small fire, shoved dirt on it, and placed a bare foot on the spot.

"Your ideas are universal. So is your struggle." Coyote spoke, almost in a whisper.

Sound of gunfire came out of the darkness and grew closer.

"The battle comes. I must go!" exclaimed the young man, a boy of sixteen really.

"The battle comes," repeated Coyote in a whisper, "and I must go."

"Adios Senor!" And with that the youth melted into the night and the sounds of battle.

"Adios, mi amigo; pobrecito." whispered Coyote to the void.

A horseman came flying over the edge of the wash, a terrifying apparition of death. Frozen like a photograph, the huge brown-spotted beast with flaring, foam-flecked nostrils, was poised in charge.

The Voice of Coyote

Astride it was a large red face, mustachios beneath flaming eyes, a pistol blazing fire at the end of a long right arm.

Bullets slammed into the earth.

November 17, 1999

as told to Doug Hodges

Coyote and the Angel

And it came to pass that the clouds roiled and turned dark and grew so heavy with water that they dropped their burden upon the land below. For days it rained and thunder drove all creatures to shelter, including Coyote. He found himself sharing a hut deep down in the Rio Grande Valley looking out at the legended river. His lone companion was different, pale and apparently sexless. Wings clung damply to its back; wings which periodically unfolded themselves into a fan seemingly three times their size, to shake and try to dry.

Other than nodding, the two followed that creed of the west that said the best said was the least said and so they said nothing. It took Coyote most of the first day to realize this creature was an Angel. He had never seen one before. This, he thought, was worth speaking about.

He sat up, scratched his left ear, and began, "I am Coyote. I have lived forever. How is it that I have never before seen an Angel?"

The voice that replied was soft and golden yet bore a strength of being; and perhaps of purpose, Coyote thought.

"I, too," the voice trickled like a mountain stream, "have been around. How is that I have never met the great Coyote? Of course, I have heard of you. You have many names."

"So! It can be too wet for even an Angel." Coyote replied, ignoring the question as his had been ignored. "Do you carry a sword? Are you an Angel of light or an Angel of dark?"

"I don't know." The melodic voice replied. The being stood up and brushed back its long hair with its hands. It looked down at itself, spreading its arms. "I don't see any weapons … and, are Angels light and dark? I'm a little muddy and damp but I seem to be more light than dark. Does that mean anything?"

"I don't know." said Coyote, somewhat perplexed. "I thought Angels were supposed to be good or bad; that they were emissaries of God or the Devil."

The Angel smiled at Coyote. "And, what do you know of the Devil, Coyote?"

"I?" exclaimed Coyote, surprised. "I know nothing. There is no Devil in my existence. For that matter, there is no good or bad. My existence is one of being, of life. I am! That is all and that is enough."

The Voice of Coyote

"Why couldn't my existence be the same?" sweetly asked the Angel.

"Well," thought Coyote, "I had heard different."

"Well," went on the Angel, "I've heard that you are the creator as well as the trickster; that you lie and kill and steal but are benevolent. How can such disparate traits belong to a single individual?"

"Easy enough." replied Coyote. "I am who I am at any given moment, in any given situation. As the time and the situation changes, so do I. Bear in mind, I am always myself ... but, always changing."

With this, Coyote lay back down.

The Angel stretched again, looked out the window at the pouring rain. The river seemed to run faster with the deluge. Definitely, the mud on the banks moved as if it had a life of its own. Of course, the Angel smiled, it does.

"It is the same with me, Coyote. I am what people perceive me to be, what they want and even demand of me. I am what I am because it is what is. And, I will be so until time comes that I change again. No one ever knows their destiny. Glory lies in the partaking."

The Angel turned to Coyote, "But, you reminded me. I must be going for I do have things to do. The rain means nothing more or less to me than it does to a flower. Good-bye, Coyote. It has been a pleasure."

With that the Angel spread its fan-like wings and was gone through the window, a ball of light moving imperviously through the air. So it seemed to Coyote, who had arisen to watch the farewell.

He waved good-bye with his paw and went back to his semi-dry corner and curled up to go back to sleep. That's one difference between us, he thought, I don't *have* to do anything, ever.

November 23, 1999

as told to Doug Hodges

Coyote As The Teacher

One day, close to the sea, a young Coyote found himself beset by followers. So, walking to the top of a small hill, he directed the animals to gather around him and he began to speak.

He spoke with tales of the Great Spirit and of the ancestors. He spoke in riddles and each animal heard him in its own language.

Coyote spoke of living, of life as now, of the path, of how to be in harmony.

Many of the animals thought Coyote's words foolish. Were they not already in harmony? After all, they were animals. They wanted to hear of how to get rid of the hated Man, and of how to find the winters less harsh, the summers less dry.

Some of the more political animals spoke out loud, interrupting Coyote with guffaws and hoots. Some even shouted angry questions and deprecations. More of the animals joined in until Coyote was forced to stop speaking.

He was appalled. Coyote had not thought of how he would be received but at the very least he had expected courtesy. He held up his paws for quiet but this only seemed to incense the crowd.

Finally, in exasperation, Coyote shut his eyes and made the animals disappear.

Coyote never really knew whether the object of his fixation disappeared or he, himself, was removed in space and time, but in any event it worked and when he opened his eyes he was alone on the small hill.

Not quite alone.

Raven sat on a nearby cactus tree, one eye cocked at Coyote.

"Haven't you learned yet, Coyote?" Raven spoke.

"No one wants to be told. No one can be told." he continued. "Everyone must learn for themselves, in their own way, in their own time."

Coyote looked at the large black bird, which was preening its feathers. How did Raven always seem to know when Coyote was having problems, always there with its own brand of preaching. It galled Coyote that Raven was usually right, to boot.

Coyote sat down and asked Raven, "Then what am I here for? Why do the animals seek me out?"

The Voice of Coyote

"You're here to be Coyote." Raven replied. "The animals seek quick fixes but they don't really want to be told anything. They want everything done."

Raven eyed Coyote again. That always made Coyote nervous. Raven's eyes were deeper than eternity and darker than the human's Hell.

"If," said Raven, "you are going to teach, it will be by example. All know you. They will see and they will learn. Or they will not."

Raven spread his wings and shook them. "You take too much time from being yourself to try to talk to them, time better spent in living. Don't be concerned for them. Each will find its own path in its own time. Harmony is all about them; they have but to live it."

With that, Raven arose, circled and was gone, flying into the west. He had seen two vultures heading that way and knew that was where he needed to be.

Scratching first his left ear, then his right, Coyote yawned. Raven was right about one thing, he was starting to worry too much.

Coyote looked about him and saw a flight of Pelican circling to dive on the near-by sea. That would be fun to watch, Coyote thought, and he trotted off in that direction.

from Raven November 30, 1999

as told to Doug Hodges

A Christmas Along the Rio Grande

i

At night, the desert is quiet and still. Some cacti raise their arms to the Moon in thanks for the coolness of the evening. Others lay low along the sandy ground, hugging the warmth left from the day. The Moon looms large, full, and shines like a crystal against a black velvet sky. Beneath its light, guided by a map of heavenly stars, a man and a pregnant mule slowly wend their way east.

The man is named Jesus Rubio. He is small in stature, looking even smaller with serape and wide-brimmed sombrero. His hair is grey, the chin and mouth bewhiskered with an unkempt beard.

Sometimes south, sometimes north of the great river, the two move along the Rio Grande, stopping here and there in this village or that. They avoid the cities. In the villages, they are well known.

It is said of the man that he does a little of everything but not a lot of anything. He helps deliver foals and calves and is said to be a speaker and healer with birds of all types. As well, it is said he has no match in the working of leather and wood.

But, his focus is on his moving; seemingly almost driven, he moves on, never staying more than a few days in any one place. The man says it is because he doesn't want to wear out his welcome. However, his acquaintances, which certainly always become his friends, say this could never happen. They all agree that he doesn't do too much but what he does do, he does very well, indeed; and that life is definitely better for his having passed through.

"Soon, Maria, soon." Jesus' quiet voice broke into the stillness of the night.

He gently pats the side of her extended belly and looks up. The sky appears to be a black bowl, filled with holes through which the radiance of heaven shines.

It had been a week, with this the seventh night, since he had heard Maria speak to him in his head. She said she wanted to go to Guerrero. And, so they started.

This was not odd for the old man had been communicating with the earth, its animals and birds, for most of his life. Sometimes, there were omens, visual images. Sometimes, the animals spoke to him, aloud or in his head. Sometimes, the Spirits came, in the earth or sky or in their animal guises. Jesus had learned long, long ago to heed the words.

Guerrero was a lost village. When they dammed the Rio Bravo it was immersed, sunken like lost Atlantis. But, with the recent years of drought, it had resurfaced, looking little worse for wear. Jesus had been born there. Now, for this seventy-fifth Christmas, he returns.

The buildings are low, made of wild local stone. He knew they would shine white in the bright sun of the day and turn gold in the afternoon. One of the cities of Cibola the conquistadors vainly searched for, he thought and chuckled.

"Come, Maria. We are here. See! She lies below and before us, a sleeping widow. Ah, what ghosts she holds."

ii

They found a house without a roof. Jesus quickly constructed one of mesquite and brush as would cover a jacal. He could still look up and see the stars but it would keep off the wind and night chill. One star, in particular, he thought, shone brighter than the others. He couldn't place it. The mind gets fuzzy at my age; he chuckled to himself.

From the riverbank, he gathered more brush and grass and made a bed for Maria who, after grazing and drinking, was ready to lie down. "Her time is very near, I think." Jesus said to himself. "I will bring water and start a fire."

The sky was alive with stars but the large one he had noticed, the one shining in the east, held prominence, its light rivaling that of the moon, which now hung high to the west.

"Day dreaming, at night, old man?" said a voice.

Jesus looked around. On top of the front wall of the house sat Eagle.

"You should be asleep at this time." the man replied.

"I should!" exclaimed the Eagle. "But, I've been sent to tell you something."

"What is that?" asked Jesus.

as told to Doug Hodges

Eagle snapped at him, "If you'll stop talking, I'll tell you."

"You're going to be visited in the next few minutes. By Spirits. These Spirits have things to impart to you."

Jesus trembled and asked, "Like yourself, friend Eagle?"

"I?" The Eagle's eyes widened. It didn't look happy.

Jesus quickly asked another question. "Is this to make me a better man?"

"Heavens, no!" cried the Eagle. "You're among the best of the humans, already."

Eagle cocked an eye, brushed a wing across its head, "It has something to do with back payments. But, I'm not clear on whose or what."

Eagle shook his head and continued, "Now, old man, time will mean nothing. You are to have no fear. Just go with the flow."

"Haven't I always?" asked Jesus.

"Yes ... well; I'm off. I need some sleep." And, with that, Eagle flew away, becoming a lighter shadow against the night sky, and was gone.

"Curious!" thought Jesus, out loud. "Well, I must go down to the river for water." He gathered up two botas and started down to the shadowy river, which he could hear in the quiet of the night. Despite its looks, the great river was and always has been alive, carrying life from the high, snowy mountains down through the rocky desert, across the lush valley to the sea. A land of treasure, of war, much death, and also much life, he thought.

He knelt down on the bank. A dead fish was at his knee. "Pobrecito! Did someone not want you or did you perhaps perish of some disease or accident. A pity for one not to fulfill their destiny. Or, maybe you have."

"Of course, he has." said a voice.

Jesus looked up. Coyote sat on the bank a little ways away, a silhouette against the moon. The man had not heard him come.

Coyote continued, "Whatever happens. That is our destiny."

Jesus sat back and stretched his legs out. "The knees just aren't what they used to be." He said.

Looking at Coyote, whose eyes shone like the stars, he asked, "But do we not have destinies to fulfill? Women much have children. Fish must be eaten. Men must fight; fight the land, the elements, each other ..."

"And what of a dead child's destiny?" asked Coyote, "Or of corn uncooked in a burning jacal? Of life, existence snuffed out or changed, like the Rio when she makes a new path?"

Coyote smiled sympathetically, "Old man, there is no destiny but life. The gift given to us all is *now*."

"Oh, there have been yesterdays as there will be tomorrows but they are not for us, as we are. They are for us as we were and as we will be."

"Give me the fish, old man. I will bless it as my dinner."

Jesus picked up the fish and tossed it to Coyote who caught it with a snap of his jaws. A couple of mighty chews, a swallow, and it was gone.

"Gracias, Senor! Vaya con Dios!" said Coyote as he raised and stretched.

"Y tu, Coyote!" Jesus watched Coyote blend into the night and disappear without apparent movement. "A strange night, this one." He muttered and proceeded to fill the botas.

iii

Maria brayed. Just once. Yet, the sound hung in the black air. She is in pain; she is alone. I must hurry to her, thought Jesus.

When he reached the shelter, it was empty. This can't be, he thought. As he looked around, a great shadow lumbered from one corner. It was Bear.

"Now I know *you* are Spirit." said Jesus. "What may I do for you?"

"I?" spoke the Bear. "I, a Spirit?" He scratched his head with one great paw. "Perhaps." The image of Bear, whose color blended with the night shadows, seemed to come and go. Jesus saw mouth, eyes, a paw, but only glimpses of an entirety.

"I'm going to sleep." It spoke as it circled round and lay down in a curled up position.

"But ... but, my Maria ... where is she? She needs me. What have you done with her?"

"What have I done?" arose Bear with a shout. "Why must it be I who have done anything?"

"She is gone." said Jesus.

"She's all right. She's still here." replied Bear.

as told to Doug Hodges

"I don't see her."

"That's because you're not in the same here as she is. Look outside."

Jesus turned around. It was day and the street was alive with people. Not looking too much different, the village now moved with life. There were curtains on the windows, hangings on the walls, tools leaning here and there.

Jesus didn't recognize any particular person but he recognized the feel. It was his Guerrero, the one where he had been a baby. He stepped out into the fresh air and pure sunlight of yesterday. People went this way and that, oblivious of him.

His eyes followed the path down to the Rio Bravo, where it danced its way along, to the coast, to the sea. It seemed bluer, clearer. Definitely, it was wider and flowed with a strength he could not remember.

"Why am I seeing this? What is there here for me?" he asked.

"Watch!" said Bear.

With the sound of the river came another. A faint wailing. Then, Jesus saw it. A baby floated in the water, being swept along by the current. "A nino!" he shouted and ran to the water's edge and wading in. The infant was bobbing like a cork and the current was swift. I'll only have one chance, thought Jesus, as he reached out one bony hand and grabbed a small arm.

"Gottcha! Por Dios!"

He waded to shore and placed the baby on the grass. It was a boy and had wisps of light colored hair. Hair and skin shone in the sunlight. A young woman came up to him and looked down over his shoulder at the baby. She whispered, "Rubio."

"Si!" Jesus said as he took off his poncho, wrapped the baby in the driest part, and handed it to the young woman.

Of a sudden, Jesus felt faint and sat down with his head between his legs. When he lifted his head, it was night. By the stars, he knew it was still the same night. "I must find Maria." And with a groan he was up and scampering toward the house.

iv

A black shadow came at him out of the night. With a kwaakk, Raven snatched away his sombrero.

The Voice of Coyote

"And what do you want, Friend Raven. I have no time for such games."

Raven flew into the dark. When it returned, it no longer bore the hat.

Raven alighted above the doorway, where Eagle had perched.

"Don't you want to know?" it said.

"Know what?" replied Jesus. "I have no time. Maria ..."

"Maria is doing what she needs to do." intoned Raven. "So must you. Pay attention!"

Jesus sighed. "Ok, Raven. What now?"

"Aren't you curious about the baby?" it asked.

"El nino? No. I'm sure the mother took care of it."

"Old man," Raven sighed, "Have you not eyes? The baby came from the river. You gave it life. You gave it its mother."

"Don't you want to know who the child was?"

"Si, Senor Raven." I'll be patient, thought Jesus. "Who was the child?"

"What did the woman say?" asked Raven.

"She said Rubio." replied Jesus. "Why, that is my name."

"And how did she know your name, old man? You were not of her time, not even of her space. She called the child Blonde, Rubio. Yes, your name."

"Ahhh!" thought Jesus.

"Was it I?" he asked. "Truly, was that my beginning? What of my true parents?"

"What of what?" Kwaakked Raven. "Is it not enough to know who you are?"

The old man stood nonplussed. Then he shook his head. "I must find Maria."

"No! Not yet. Tonight, you must ... be." Raven spread its dark wings and arose to blend into the black above. The old man's hat fell out of the sky to the ground. Jesus picked it up and went back into the house.

v

The inside of the house was there no longer. Jesus placed his hands on the stone sides of the doorway. Before him gaped a huge prairie, open and stretching out as far as he could see, under a bright

as told to Doug Hodges

sun and an endless blue sky. In the distance he could see a rolling cloud, small, but steadily growing. There was the sound of constant thunder.

The cloud was low to the horizon and spread out as it got larger. Before his eyes, it moved like a creature alive, which, Jesus saw, was just what it was. Not a single creature but a massive herd of thousands of Buffalo, moving as one across the vast expanse; a herd that must of existed in his grandfather's or perhaps his great-grandfather's time.

The herd, in thunder and dust, grew monstrous before his eyes and when Jesus thought it would trample over him as if he weren't even there, it turned, again, as if a single beast, and rushed madly by.

The scene had been awe-inspiring and Jesus was breathless, numbed. He stared at the ground, trampled and torn, tilled more efficiently than by any plow. He looked up. Buffalo stood before him. Huge and looming, maybe seven or eight feet, it stood aright. One half of Buffalo was a brown so dark as to almost be black. The other side was as white as a lamb. Jesus could not tear his eyes away but he nodded. "Buffalo. I greet you."

"And I, you, hombre." replied Buffalo. "Do you know when you are?"

"A long time ago." answered Jesus.

"Si. Only Prairie Dog lives in larger numbers and they aren't nomadic. My people roam from the mountains in the west to the great river in the east, from the land of many waters in the north to the great river in the south. We have life and death but no fear. It is as if nothing can truly harm us. Yet, in a moment, our lack of fear almost caused our extinction. It was said we would be lost por siempre. But, like others which human beings deem 'lesser,' we go on. The cycle goes around."

It shook its shaggy head, "It really makes no difference if we were gone in body, you know. For we came and were a part of the all; as such a thread woven into the blanket of time.

Jesus asked, "And, what do you have to say to me?"

"Say!" Buffalo replied, "I have nothing to say. None of us have. It is you, my friend, who must see and hear if you are to learn."

The Voice of Coyote

vi

The night returned. Maria was giving birth. Jesus watched, thinking he should comfort her and yet all was well; an action immemorial, a scene played out a million times, and many more, without consulting him.

Mother was nuzzling and cleaning the infant, a fine male. The two, an image of softness and hope in the flickering light of the small fire. When had he built that? he wondered.

"Sooo …" came a voice from the ceiling. On a branch sat Owl. Like Bear, he was indistinct, seen more in the blotting out of sky and shadow than an actual form.

"Si, Brother Owl. So, indeed. A strange night … yet, a wondrous one, I think." Said Jesus. "Are you here to teach me something?"

"Whooo would I teach, Senor? We are all here to learn … por siempre. We are all here to teach, likewise. But, there must be eyes to see, ears to hear."

"I am here." said Jesus. "I am always here."

"Sooo you are. Would you heed me?"

"Of a certainty, unto death. Yet, Raven mentioned nothing of gaining my soul. Eagle said to have no fear and I have none. I have never feared death, anyway. But, I would worry about Maria and her new little one."

"Ooohh, I'm not here for that. You may not fear death but you are preoccupied with it. It will come when it does, to all. Even contemplating death wastes energy better put elsewhere."

With that Owl stretched, his wings moving outward an incredible distance. "Yooouu belong with mankind. You are a gift to your own. A gift of teaching, if you will. A gift of life and love, a sounding board, a tuning pipe, a wellspring to nourish …"

"I am but an old man, Senor Owl. I know nothing of what you say."

"Oooff course not. And you need not know. Know only that that is where you now belong. The gift of life has been given to you as it is yours to give to others." Owl arose as a giant shadow and swooped down and through the door, Jesus having to swiftly duck.

as told to Doug Hodges

vii

The sun was shining high and brightly in the cloudless sky when they left Guerrero, the man and two mules. They headed south towards Nuevo Guerrero.

They rested on a rise above the Rio Grande, Jesus patted Maria and then the newcomer to whom the name El Sol was given. Perhaps it will be good to stop traveling so much, hey mules, he thought. The two mules looked at him and brayed. Then Maria returned to her grazing and El Sol returned to his nursing.

from El Rio Bravo
(for SoloSpeak and our first Christmas, 1999)

The Voice of Coyote

Coyote and The Cross

Coyote was wandering down across the great expanse called Texas, having left the Panhandle and heading toward the Hill Country, when he spied, a great distance off, a great shiny cross. Though it was on a slight hill, it was still so large that it could be seen for miles. Coyote sat down, scratched behind his left ear with his hind left paw, and decided he'd investigate.

Before him, The Cross, as the sign proclaimed it to be, rose 80 feet into the Texas sky, a glittering thing of metal plates and bolts, rather than the solid surface he had first thought.

Its four points were equal in length and the whole structure, star, beams, and base, was solid shiny steel. It rested upon a concrete pad and at the base, going around the four sides, were a picture of Jesus and images of the Catholic Stations of the Cross.

Coyote sat off to one side in the shade of a Hackberry tree (or so he thought; other than to mark territory, Coyote didn't pay too much attention to trees) and wondered why Man would go to such trouble to erect such a monument. It seemed such a grand gesture, apparently impervious to the pernicious Texas weather, and not at all functional, as far as Coyote could tell. And, he had learned that little was done by Man which didn't perform some sort of function, usually for his own physical and/or financial betterment.

Coyote sat pondering and scratching fleas when a brand new, shiny white, one-ton pick-up truck drove up in a cloud of Texas dust.

The first man literally jumped out of the cab and, ohhing and ahhing, began snapping pictures from a very expensive and professional-looking camera. He was young, and wore a journalist's vest crammed with lenses, film, notepads and such paraphernalia.

From the other side, the driver's side, emerged an elderly gentleman. A 'Texan,' Coyote knew immediately. It wasn't only the immaculately white Stetson, the long black bolo that ran down his chest, or even the polished and hand-sewn boots into which his pants were tucked, that bespoke this. It was his manner; crinkled eyes that gazed at The Cross in awe, the weathered hand which took off the hat as another shielded those eyes, eyes as old as Texas, as wild as the wind, as young as the rushing river waters. He stood short but erect, humble yet proud, and spoke with a softness that could be heard

as told to Doug Hodges

above the wind and birds (and more likely oil derricks or lowing cattle, thought Coyote).

Coyote recognized him as one of those pioneers which intrepidly fought Indians and weather and the land to scratch out an existence in the Texas soil; or those who ran more than half-wild cattle through the chaparral and mesquite, across swollen rivers, fighting off rustlers of all races and types; or yet one of those who burrowed and drilled into that earth in search of riches or one sort or another.

The older man had corralled the younger and, paper and pen in hand, the youngster began to write while the elder related his tale.

Coyote listened patiently. That was the way to learn. It seemed the old man was a rich oil 'Baron' and that he and another elderly man had been in the hospital together at death's door. The other man said that he wanted to place crosses across Texas but then he died. The old oilman miraculously lived and decided to dedicate his fortune and the rest of his life in performing that task.

Coyote walked up to the two, sat down, and said, "Excuse me. But, what is it for?"

The old man looked at Coyote and took off his hat, "Why, it's to remind us of our Savior, He who died to save us all from sin and give us hope in the resurrection."

"Well," said Coyote, "I'm all for hope."

"This is sort of an out of the way spot," he observed, "why here?"

"Well," the old man replied, "this is the first one. Actually, this is a cross-roads, though maybe no freeways go through. A lot of people do."

"Eventually, we want to put them on all the major thoroughfares of Texas; four in the Dallas/Ft. Worth area, the most sinful area, and one in El Paso. I think we'll try that one next."

"But," continued Coyote, "what does it do, exactly?"

"Why, the cross is the symbol of Jesus Christ, the Son of God, made Man," The old man replied, "who came and lived on earth, was betrayed and crucified, and died to save us all from sin."

"What is sin," asked Coyote?

"Sin?" the old man was taken aback. "Sin ... is breaking God's law, committing actions one knows are wrong."

Coyote asked, "Like what?"

"Ummm ... like murder, for one." said the man. "Or breaking any of the ten commandments, such as stealing, adultery ..."

The Voice of Coyote

"I got you!" said Coyote. "Things that throw the path of life out of harmony."

"I guess that's one way of puttin' it."

Coyote was still puzzled. "But, what did the crucifixion of this ... this, Jesus, have to do with 'sins?'"

"Well, I'm not a priest or a preacher but I'll give it a whirl." The old man looked at the cross and took a deep breath. "Jesus Christ was the innocent Son of God, God made Man, born of a virgin. He was the Lamb whose blood washes away the sins of the world; the sacrificial lamb, who was betrayed and killed by Man ... to forgive all of our sins, so that we might all have eternal life."

Coyote scratched his ear. "You already live."

"Yes. But, through Christ, we will live forever in Heaven."

"Heaven?" another new concept to Coyote. "What is Heaven?"

"After death," said the old man, "all who are in God's grace go to Heaven, a place of purity and light, to be with all the saints and angels and Jesus Christ and God."

"And ..." asked Coyote, "if one does not die in God's grace?"

The old man shook his head and said, "They go to Hell."

"What is Hell," asked Coyote?

"For someone who gets around a lot, you don't know much about the Lord. Haven't you ever read the Bible?"

"I don't read the words of Man." Said Coyote. "Nothing personal."

"Oh! Well, Hell is a place of darkness, eternal damnation; it's a place of fire and brimstone and eternal chaos."

"That would be Hell all right." Said Coyote. "I think I understand, now."

"Thank you very much, sir. I wish you all the best in your endeavors. I must move on now. Adios!"

"God bless you for stopping by, Coyote." waved the man.

"Oh, he did." replied Coyote over his shoulder. 'And he does.' thought Coyote as he trotted down the road. Humans lived things so complicated but interesting. Coyote prayed, 'May your dreams live as large as your heart, old man.'

March, 2000

as told to Doug Hodges

'Foxy' Morning

O'le Coyote was feeling pretty 'foxy' early one morning, if you'll excuse the expression. He ran to the top of a sandy dune overlooking the shipping canal leading into and out of South Texas. There, he watched the shrimp boats sail out into the golden horizon.

As, he followed the canal to the sea, he thought, 'Fish would be nice for breakfast.' And he trotted down the beach.

Sea gulls flitted here and there, diving and circling and generally being as boisterous as possible. A small squadron of pelicans was offshore a short distance taking turns diving into the waves.

Coyote sat down and looked around. Sand fleas were hopping; he unconsciously began to scratch.

Then he saw just the one he was looking for.

He ran to the jetties, a row of huge stones designating the mouth of the shipping channel. Another row could be seen on the opposite shore. Here, he carefully, for they were wet and slippery from the ocean's spray, made his way to the end.

Sliding in and out of the waves, leaping and gamboling in the sun, was Dolphin and his mate.

"Friend Dolphin," cried Coyote, when they happened close by.

"Hola Coyote!" they both cried. And, Dolphin asked, "Como esta?"

"Muy bien, gracias!" replied Coyote. "But, I'm a little hungry and was wondering if you might catch and toss me a fish."

"Ahhh," said Dolphin, "I, myself, was wondering what it was you were wanting. Of a certainty. Un momento, por favor." And Dolphin, with a great leap out of the water, dived and was gone. His mate looked at Coyote and shook her head before she, too, disappeared. Coyote apparently didn't notice.

Now Dolphin, who was also feeling 'foxy' this morning, if you'll excuse the expression, thought he'd play a prank on Coyote. Was not Coyote always asking favors? Actually, it seemed the only time anyone saw Coyote was when he wanted something, even if it was only one's attention.

Dophin scooped up a nice redfish but also nosed a small, somewhat irate, crab into the fish's mouth. 'This should be good,' he thought.

"Hola, Coyote! Catch!"

Coyote caught the fish in his solid jaws and began to swallow.

Yes, Coyote's mother *had* told him to chew his food; but, as with all the good advice he'd been given over the years, Coyote chose to forget it and do things his own way.

The fish was starting to slide down the throat when Coyote felt something ... strange ... pulling on the back of his tongue ... seemingly pulling itself up towards the mouth.

He quickly snapped his jaw shut. He heard a tapping on the inside of his teeth.

With a gulp, Coyote finished swallowing the fish. The tapping continued.

"Whooosh der?" Coyote attempted to ask without opening his mouth.

"None a your business, senor." Came a small reply from inside.

"Ged outda my moth." Mumbled Coyote.

"Impossible!" replied the distinctive Latin voice. "Your mouth, she is closed. But, I fix. Un momento, por favor."

Coyote sat ... waiting. He knew something was going to happen but didn't know what. He didn't think he wanted to find out either.

"Yeeooowwww!" screeched Coyote. His mouth opened and out shot Crab.

A tiny voice could be heard, "Free at last! Thank the Sea, I'm free at last!"

Crab landed like a skimming rock. When he stopped on the beach, he sidled his way back towards Coyote, who walked to meet him.

Crab glared. "You just watch out who you're eatin' in the future. Comprende?"

Coyote nodded his head.

With a jerk of the head, the crustacean crabbed off sideways down the beach and into the surf.

Coyote sat. He sat for a long time staring at where Crab had disappeared. He no longer felt 'foxy.' Now, he felt 'sheepish.'

Dolphin drifted by once, twice, again and again, then finally hollered, "And how was breakfast, Senor Coyote?"

Coyote looked at him and then started laughing. He laughed and laughed, rolling about in the sand, oblivious of the fleas, sand crabs, or the lapping tide.

as told to Doug Hodges

Eventually, Coyote composed himself enough to answer, "A fine breakfast, friend Dolphin. Muchas gracias!"

Coyote arose and shook the sand from his fur. "I'll have to do you a good turn, sometime." He cried. "Buenas dias, amigo! And to the missus!"

He trotted back to the sandy dune where he had set earlier. The shrimp boats were gone. The day was alive and bright, very warm with a humid breeze.

Coyote chuckled. 'Aye,' he thought to himself, 'there's a lesson in all of this.'

He shook his head, 'But right now, I'm still hungry.' And Coyote followed the channel inland to the west.

April 6, 2000

Coyote's Plan

Coyote sat on a slight rise above the highway. Large trucks, from both sides of the border, whizzed passed. An seemingly endless stream of cars ... 'So many people,' Coyote thought, 'going so many places.'

He shook his head. It all made him dizzy. 'But, it's not the people.' He thought. After all, he had helped create them. 'It's the metal monsters they've created. They strip away all sense of propriety, of rhythm and peace. Now, if they could be removed ...'

"Electricity!" he exclaimed. Coyote arose and began to pace back and forth, furiously thinking. 'All their so-called civilization is based on electricity. Stop it and they will have to return to nature, to the rhythm of the earth.'

And it came to pass. One day, there was no electricity. Cars wouldn't start, nor trucks nor motorcycles. For that matter, neither was there any heating, air conditioning. It was a traumatic time for man. Even Coyote winced at their trials. Thousands died, maybe a million lives, before things settled down into some sort of normalcy.

Steam trains, and even cars, came back briefly, as did the use of animals for transportation. Wood- and charcoal-burning stoves and heaters, and viaducts for water and waste, were once more in vogue. Man's road of civilization slipped back a hundred years or so. But, it was a mere slip, not a fall.

Within five years, water power had been harnessed as a direct power source; within ten, so had the sun and wind, the very ether, not as a prelude to something else (as had been the case with electricity) but as sources unique and distinct in themselves. Man's trek, again, zoomed by incredibly.

Coyote sat on a slight hill overlooking the highway. A steady stream of vehicles, trucks and cars and motorbikes, of one sort and another, flowed below him. True, they were now powered differently, the smell and sound different, but the image was virtually unchanged from before. The hurry, hurry and chaotic mass movement had ceased but for the blinking of an eye.

Coyote sighed deeply, shook his head, lay down with his head on his paws and went to sleep.

May 11, 2000

as told to Doug Hodges

Coyote at the Hospital

Coyote felt uneasy. The hair on his neck and back stood on end. The building smelled of medicine, pain and death. Spirits flittered here and there in a perpetual state of agitation and there was no peace.

Coyote found himself at the bedside of an old man. An indeterminate age, the man's body was frail; he seemed emaciated and an oxygen tube rested below his nose. From a man-made tree hung an IV attached to one bony arm with a long needle and tape.

Only the man's eyes seemed young, alive and moving.

"Hey Coyote!" the man said in a raspy voice. "What brings you here?"

"I hardly know." Replied Coyote.

He peered closely into the man's face. "Do I know you?"

"You should." Chuckled the man. "Once I was first man."

"Ahhh!" said Coyote. He then asked, "And why am I here?"

"Because I'm going to die." Said the man.

Coyote started. "What has that to do with me?" he exclaimed. "Men die!"

"So do Coyotes." The man replied.

"But …" Coyote slowly spoke with a smile, "Coyote never dies."

The man stared at Coyote, cocked an eye, "Neither does Man."

He strained to go on, "Man is no less a part of the plan than yourself. Perhaps more so." The man coughed and wheezed, lost his breath, then paused.

When he was breathing regularly again, the old man continued. "Despite his conscious loss of spiritual path, his ignorance at understanding, man is still an integral part of the circle of life."

He sighed. "Often, he forgets."

The man paused a moment and stared. "Sometimes you and the other Spirits forget."

"You want to know why you are here, Coyote?" asked the man. Coyote nodded. "You are here that I may go in harmony. You are here that we may transcend together."

Coyote thought, 'I need no transition.' He asked, "What has Man … what have you to do with me?"

The man sighed, again, heavily. "It is in man's perception that you have strengthened and prospered. Without man there would be no

The Voice of Coyote

lessons to be learned ... no need of any lessons. You, Coyote, and the others would not be needed."

Coyote thought about that. He had never thought of himself as a teacher. Actually, he never thought of himself as *being* much of anything. He was 'Coyote.' That was all there was. That was all he needed.

The man reached out with a claw-like hand and grasped the mane on Coyote's neck. A machine began a steady high-pitched whine.

His last breath came out, "We are and ever more shall be."

The man was gone. So was Coyote.

High on a hill, Coyote sat and watched a group of native children running around cactus and through stands of cane. Birds sang and flew about. A small herd of deer grazed on the periphery.

He arose and started down, to be closer to the laughter.

A gun shot rang out, echoing with a steady high-pitched whine.

The children disappeared along with the birds and wildlife. Javalina could be heard scurrying through the cane.

Coyote, too, melted into the now silent earth.

June 8, 2000

as told to Doug Hodges

The End of The River

It was a February morning and the mist was thick as El Perro de Dios, God's Dog, better known as Coyote, was winding his way along the Rio Grande east of Brownsville. The river seemed shallow and slow as it wound its way but Coyote knew that was an illusion. Too many poor souls had found that out the hard way and drowned. Still, it was not the mighty Grande that it had been in the days of the steamboats. Drought, dams, irrigation and the general machinations of man has seen to that.

On this day, a strange phenomena brought Coyote up short. There, where the Rio usually ran into the Gulf of Mexico, and the salty waters of the sea, lay a sand bar. A good fifty yards of sand continued the beach from one country to another. The waters of the Rio trickled left and right into tiny tributaries and onto salt pans but could not muster enough energy to assail the wide dune of sand.

Two Border Patrol vehicles sat like waiting gulls and red markers were set up designating borders that no longer had a physical delineation.

Coyote could not remember seeing such a thing, though a passing Pelican said it had happened once before, some 50 years ago, in a drought.

Coyote lay on a brushy dune and watched. For a week he lay there, observing. The Rio Grande grew no more bold, though the trickling waters filled the salt pans into small shallow seas. And, another strange phenomena occurred.

As if on a pilgrimage … "Exactly!" thought Coyote … hundreds of people flocked to see the blockage of the river. A continuous procession of vehicles moved up and down the beach on both sides of the border. Young and old, men, women and children, rich and poor, gathered to stare in awe. Some, like Coyote, seemed saddened; some came with a carnival atmosphere and these reminded him of the people queuing up to see the dead bodies lined up during the border war. Most just came to witness a unique event, making no judgment.

One morning as he watched, part of a long forgotten poem came to Coyote's mind:

"'If seven maids with seven mops
Swept it for half a year,

The Voice of Coyote

Do you suppose,' the Walrus said,
'That they could get it clear?'
'I doubt it,' said the Carpenter,
And shed a bitter tear."*

Coyote mentioned this to the Pelican, who kept coming back to him for conversation. "Why would anyone want to do that?" it replied.

'A good enough response.' thought Coyote.

Finally Coyote got bored, and being bored, remembered he was hungry.

He arose and stretched, thanked the Great Spirit for this latest of mysteries and trod off. Perhaps, he would visit The Island, he thought when another line of verse entered his head, unbidden:

"I'll tell thee everything I can;
There's little to relate.
I saw an aged aged man,
A-sitting on a gate.
'Who are you aged man?' I said.
'And how is it you live?'
And his answer trickled though my head
Like water through a sieve."*

Coyote laughed and laughed.

The Pelican, cocking his head, could still hear Coyote long after he was lost from view.

February 15, 2001
* *quoted from* <u>Through The Looking Glass</u> *by Lewis Carroll*

as told to Doug Hodges

Coyote and Roadrunner

Coyote lay on a semi-grassy knoll one day, alone and feeling dejected. It was an illusion he knew; so much of life was. But, the path of life also hinges on emotion. So, he figured he should do something about the feeling.

He sat up and scanned the desert before him. 'I'll have a party,' he thought.

At that moment, Roadrunner trotted by. 'And, I'll invite Roadrunner.'

Now, Roadrunner and Coyote had a unique, to say the least, friendship. Coyote had no enemies to speak of and was pretty much liked, at least tolerated, by everyone. When in Roadrunner's company, he was always polite and entertaining. Roadrunner, on the other hand, did have a problem with Coyote's propensity to eat her young.

But, at this time, Roadrunner was living alone in her nest and so decided to accept Coyote's invitation to his party. She *had* asked if anyone else would be there. The last time she and Coyote had gone on a date, it was an Eagle's concert, he had put the moves on her and she was not entirely sure how that had made her feel.

"Oh sure," said Coyote, "lots of folk. I'm inviting everybody."

But, everybody didn't come.

The drought had played havoc with schedules. The deer were out foraging, Hawk, Mouse, and Rabbit were frantically trying to feed their families, even Armadillo was considering moving his people up north due to the lack of food.

Then, Fox, Possum, Eagle and Skunk were at the weekly poker game, "How could you forget?"

Thus, when the time came that evening, only Roadrunner appeared at Coyote's cabin door.

"Hi Kid." Coyote said, as Roadrunner entered. She looked around at the single room with loft. 'Busy' was not even the word for what she saw. Every bit of wall space was covered with something, a photograph, newspaper clipping, drawing, recipe, sign, article of clothing. The floor was full of stuff, some of which was furniture.

"Nothing's changed." Said Roadrunner, "Maybe some new cobwebs and mouse droppings."

The Voice of Coyote

"Ouch!" replied Coyote. "Was that nice?"

"Maybe not. Where's everybody?" she asked.

"They couldn't make it." Roadrunners eyebrows rose. "Honest! I really tried. Here, have a seat." And Coyote whisked a pile of books off of what could have been a bed or a sofa with no back or a table or most anything.

Roadrunner sat gingerly and sighed. "OK, what's on the agenda?"

It wasn't long before Roadrunner was contentedly fed, a surprising vegetarian grill, and leaning back against some sort of fur piece hanging on the wall, eyes closed, a glass of Chablis in her hand, the soft light from candles playing against her eyelids, with Elvis and Sinatra wafting gently in the background.

She opened one eye and saw Coyote lying on the floor, legs casually draped over what could have been a rock but was probably a pile of books. His eyes were closed as he gently hummed to 'My Way'. "Isn't it always." She murmured.

"What was that, Querida?" questioned Coyote.

"Nothing!" sighed Roadrunner. "You're just too damn good at this."

Just after dawn, with a smile and a kiss, Roadrunner left. Coyote, who had been sitting outside the door watching the sunrise, smiled back, stood up and waved as she drove out of sight in her vintage Austin Healey. Her horn responded with a quick "beep-beep."

As always, Coyote felt renewed by the night's company and the coming morning; he felt awe, humbled, alive and purposeful all at the same time. He shook his head as he watched Eagle flying home against the rising sun.

'Time for breakfast.' he thought.

Reflections
August 8, 2001

as told to Doug Hodges

An Unkindness Of Ravens

Raven was on tour with the band. They were somewhere west of Omaha, in an early morning of the great nowhere, when the bus broke down.

Raven told Coyote, who was driver, mechanic, instrument polisher, tuner, sometimes bass player, and general go-fer for the band, to fix it. Coyote looked at the shiny black beast, which was resting on a slight angle in the dry, unkempt grass on the side of the road. He thought disgustedly, 'Of course it was a back road; no interstate for An Unkindness Of Ravens. We're seeing America.'

Coyote scratched his head, walked around the bus like he had never seen it before, crawled underneath, it, found a spot where nothing leaked on him, curled up and went to sleep.

Raven, meanwhile, had grabbed a guitar and made his way to a lonely knoll which bore a single large shade tree; 'Perhaps a Joshua.' he thought. There he settled and begin to pick and strum. The rest of the band, five members of Raven's family, flew off to do their own thing. The sun rose and made its way high into the cloudless sky.

Raven was picking out a new tune and humming along, searching for words. He had never had word problems before but of late, they were shy and elusive.

Then he noticed that, except for himself, there was not a sound; no birds, no wind, no planes, no vehicles, no sounds of repair.

With a deep sigh, Raven walked back to the bus and looked underneath.

He found a stick and poked Coyote awake.

"Is it fixed?" asked Raven.

"Sure!" replied Coyote. "Wha cha think I know about these mechanical contraptions? I dream fixed it."

"Really!" exclaimed Raven, "Can you do that?"

"Dun it!" said Coyote.

Raven called the band together with as loud, "Kwaaakkk!" They saddled up, Coyote fired up the diesel and was only a little surprised as they smoothly moved on down the road.

* * * * * * *

Vegas! Land of Elvis, aging singers, empty pockets, a sadistic Disneyland for adults …

The Voice of Coyote

An Unkindness Of Ravens was playing The Riviera. Raven strutted and twanged his way back and forth across the stage; the room rocked with sound and movement. The last song, where the lights went out and hundreds of tiny flames lit the man-made night, was especially moving.

Coyote yawned.

With a last, "Luv ya!" Raven bowed his way off the stage. The band folded their tents and prepared to steal away into the real night.

"That was perfect, Raven." Coyote commented. "You almost couldn't hear the gazillion slot machines in the background."

"What are you on about, Coyote? It was a good concert." responded Raven. "Just clean the instruments and pack them up. And let's get out of here."

'Ah, fleeing the scene of the crime.' thought Coyote. But, it was useless to bait Raven. The two had discussed, rehashed and argued it all too many times. Raven just didn't get that music was a gift from the Great Spirit to be shared freely, not sold in glittering palaces ... even the cheap and tarnished ones where they too often found themselves.

* * * * * * *

They were again on a back road, this time in New Mexico, cutting south from Colorado. Raven was surprised when they broke down in Chaco Canyon. Not surprised that they broke down ... 'Sometimes I think Coyote does that on purpose.' he thought ... but that they were in Chaco.

He had not been here, literally, in ages; not since man had dwelt here, building his small communal structures up and down the sides of the canyon. Not since Raven, himself, had been worshipped and prayed to. And, the thought being dredged up unbidden, not since Raven had truly felt like he was a worthwhile part of existence.

Raven glared at Coyote as the others wandered off. "You did this on purpose!" he accused.

"Me!" exclaimed Coyote. "What do you think I am, a magician or something?"

'Exactly!' thought Raven. 'Exactly!' Instead, he glared and asked, How long this time?"

"Seems pretty bad." said Coyote, as he threw up the hood and the radiator, on cue, blew like Old Faithful. "Overnight, at least."

as told to Doug Hodges

Raven sighed.

* * * * * * *

Raven and the others sat around the campfire Coyote had built. Raven had his guitar in hand and was strumming softly. He pondered his lack of words.

Coyote picked up the acoustic bass and started a beat; the others joined in. Even without electronics, the sound arose, moved up and around and through the canyon, reaching up to the very stars flooding the ceiling sky.

The ghosts came then and sang along with An Unkindness Of Ravens; sang without words and with words long unheard and forgotten. They sang with tears, with blood, with fear, with anger and with passion.

All the creatures of the desert came, now, animal, bird, insect, reptile, and even man; and they listened as they sat and lay side by side. It was a remarkable time of Spirit, unheard of in any of their lifetimes. Eventually all were singing, dancing, sounding in a song of harmony and life.

The concert went on until the Sun was fully up and prayers of thanksgiving for the old and for the new were woven into the song.

Then, suddenly, it was over.

An Unkindness Of Ravens looked around at the empty, desolate ruins, baking in the desert sun, and began to put their instruments away.

"Can we go now, Coyote?" asked Raven.

"Whenever." Coyote replied, trying not to smile.

"Fine!" Raven said, starting to move away. He turned, "Coyote, let's go up to the northwest, by the ocean. We can sing on the rocks to the denizens of the sea and the coast."

"No more concert halls?" asked Coyote.

"Not for awhile." smiled Raven.

November 23, 2001

The Voice of Coyote

Coyote Goes To Heaven

As is his wont, one day Coyote wandered aimlessly along when he came to a deep valley, all in white cloud. Clouds rose up all about and surrounded the valley like a snowy comforter. At the entrance rose a great arched gate, made of gold and encrusted with pearls. Coyote could see a road, paved with gold, leading off into a golden city, buildings and towers, interspersed with whip-cream-like clouds.

Leaning against the right-hand side of the gate was a tall, slim figure with long brown hair and beard, wearing a white robe stitched with gold. It was Saint Peter.

"Hi Pete!" said Coyote.

"Lo, Coyote!" replied Saint Peter.

"Some digs you got here." said Coyote.

"We like it." came the reply.

"Don't suppose you'd let me take a look inside?" asked Coyote, quietly.

"Ya know better than that." replied the bearded Saint. "Heaven ain't for the likes o' you."

"Sure enough, this is not exactly my idea of Heaven." Coyote grinned what he thought was his winningest smile, "Still, I'd like to take a look."

"Nope Coyote. Got strict orders. 'Specially for you. Sorry!" said Pete.

"That's OK." replied Coyote nonchalantly. "I understand completely. No hard feelings. Peace, Brother!" With a wave, Coyote was off. Saint Peter waved also, thinking to himself, 'That was too easy ...?'

Around the cloudy hill Coyote started climbing, angling up and around. There wasn't a fence as such, just the gate and seemingly impossibly high hills, encircling the valley. Then, Coyote started to dig, right through the cloud.

After what seemed a long time, Coyote poked his head out into the white, fluffy valley of Heaven.

First, he saw people moving along, gliding rather than walking, and they all wore white sheets and had wings on the backs of their shoulders. Other than that, they looked like normal humans, men and women. 'The dead who believe in this Heaven,' thought Coyote.

as told to Doug Hodges

Coyote transformed himself to look like these, with white sheet and wings. It was hard to hide his ears but Coyote gave himself a lot of hair in a pompadour. And then he, too, walked around.

Here and there Coyote saw, angels. They differed from the humans in that they hovered above the ground and were a white gold rather than milk-appearing. They all had long polished hair and seemed sexless. They also seemed more alert, more purposeful, than the humans who seemed dazed or lackadaisical.

No one seemed to be doing much of anything, as far as Coyote could tell, neither the aimless humans nor the intent angels.

As he worked his way through the golden streets, Coyote saw thousands upon thousands of humans and hundreds of angels. All the buildings seemed to arch and lead to great towering spires. Everything seemed to be made of cloud. At times Coyote couldn't even see his feet. Yet, the buildings appeared substantial enough and were decorated with an endless stream of rich gems and stones and, of course, gold. The gold was warm and smooth to his touch.

He wove around and around, ever inward, aiming towards the center of the great golden city, which seemed to sit upon a slight hill. Here, steep spires arose everywhere; great golden arches that were definitely not MacDonald's or the city of St. Louis.

As Coyote came closer to the center, it didn't seem possible, it got whiter and brighter, like walking into a light bulb or the sun, itself.

At the very center, Coyote found himself in a gigantic cathedral room. Here, there were no pews, no chairs, no alter, no decorations, no balconies, only an immense space of light floating upwards and out. Without actually hearing it, Coyote could sense a wonderous music, feel the rhythm pulsate though his blood. All was void and at peace. The sensation was of absolutely nothing, at once hypnotic and addictive.

The voice spoke, **"Hello Coyote!"**

"Hello!" replied Coyote. Unconsciously, he transformed into his normal flea-bitten appearance. "I hope you're not too upset with my coming."

"Of course not;" The voice replied. **"I've always expected you."** A pause, and then, **"You're always welcome."**

"But, the gate?" said Coyote. "Peter said ..."

"Just a joke." came the voice. **"A joke among ... gods ... friends, I mean."**

The Voice of Coyote

"Yeah, sure." said Coyote, unsure of himself. That bothered him. He was never unsure of himself and almost always had a quick retort for any occasion.

"Well, I've got to be going. Nice place!" said Coyote.

"We like it." came the voice.

"Peace!" said Coyote and he turned to leave.

"And, Peace be with you!" replied the voice.

Thinking, 'That was strange!' Coyote wander back through the streets, this time looking like his normal self. People stared. Some hid. Some crossed their forefingers. All whispered. The angels appeared to glare and the hair on Coyotes back bristled.

So, it was a relief when he came to the back side of the great golden gate. Saint Peter was waiting for him.

"Boss said ya was comin' through. Mind tellin' me how ya got in?"

"Trade secret." Winked Coyote. And he trotted away from heaven as fast as he could and still keep a semblance of dignity.

June, 2002

as told to Doug Hodges

Coyote And The Favor or What's A Miracle Between Friends

Coyote is nobody's fool but his own. So, when Raven came to him and asked a favor (Raven never asked for favors) Coyote thought to himself, 'It must be a trick of some kind!' and he readily accepted.

Raven said he had inadvertently promised the Great Spirit two miracles, in two different places, at the same time. The first was to a group of children in a small desert town in western Texas, along the border. They had never seen snow, nor had many even heard of it. There was drought and the heat beat unmercifully and they envisioned a blanket of white purity, a moment of relief, of hope and renewal, a miracle. Thus, they prayed. The second was to a fishing village up along the northwest coast of Canada. The fish had stopped coming and the village's livelihood, its very existence, was threatened.

Coyote thought and said, "I'll do the kids. I'm better with children than you." Raven glared at Coyote but acknowledged to himself that it was true. Coyote's simplistic attitude always struck a chord with the young. Besides, that was the miracle Raven had intended Coyote to tackle anyway. How could even Coyote screw that one up?

So it came to pass that Coyote appeared in the dusty streets of a tiny western town, surrounded by a small herd of children. Out on the fringes hung a number of adults, burros, dogs and the other requisite denizens of small towns everywhere.

Coyote sat and scratched behind his left ear. "So, you want snow, huh?"

"Oh, si, Senor Coyote! Por favor!" replied one little gamin. Coyote couldn't tell if it was a boy or a girl but figured it had to be a girl. Boys were usually too shy.

"It will get cold." Said Coyote, "Then melt and turn all this dust to mud."

The herd just stared wide-eyed. Coyote shifted to scratching the right ear.

Then the urge came over him all of a sudden and Coyote began scratching and scratching and white flakes flew from his pelt until

The Voice of Coyote

they began to fill the air. In a moment the sky was filled with large white flakes gently floating and settling to the ground.

The children stood transfixed, with open mouths and rapt expressions. It *was* snow. Tongues stuck out to taste the miracle. Many knelt and bowed their heads. But for a moment, then were up making snow balls, lying down and forming snow angels, throwing handfuls of the white miracle on each others heads.

Even the adults were dumb-struck and stared. Some fingered their beads in prayer, others became as the children and began to play.

Just as the children were starting to feel the cold, the sky cleared and the snow stopped. Within an hour, except for one or two snowballs hastily placed into a box and sunk into the river, and that scooped into containers by the adults for water, the miracle was over. Yet, it would be spoken of for generations upon generations; the day snow came to the desert. It would never be forgotten.

Interestingly enough, though, Coyote's presence would be forgotten. In later years, only one old woman would remember that he had been there and might have had something to do with the miracle. Then, eventually, even that memory would be gone.

Raven's miracle was somewhat harder. Nature was out of harmony. Too much easy fishing had decimated the fish population down the river and at the inlet to the sea. To make things worse, whale hunters had driven the whales south to the village's fishing grounds. So, Raven prayed for harmony and asked the Great Spirit for a path.

Suddenly, Raven was tired and he settled upon a mound of earth. The mound seethed beneath him, roiled and moved; an earthquake was born. The earth formed a finger out of the mouth of the river and thrust it into the sea, creating a jetty and forming coves to each side. New streams came forth, streams not known by man.

Now the fish would come back, or rather be allowed to grow again. The whales would stop and be content on the northern side of the jetty. The village lay on the south.

Raven was worshipped. His image carved into the top of totem poles. Long, long after the memory of this miracle had faded from mankind, Raven would continue to be revered.

"Everything go OK?" asked Raven of Coyote.

"Sure!" replied Coyote. "They never even knew I was there."

"Ahh!" That's just what Raven had hoped for.

as told to Doug Hodges

July, 2002

The Voice of Coyote

Idioms

An Unkindness Of Ravens was playing a roadhouse out of the one-horse town of Langtry, Texas. There was quite a crowd as folk had come from, literally, miles around, even as far off as Sanderson and Del Rio.

Earlier in the day, the band was having breakfast in the town's small café. Coyote was having biscuits and gravy, to him, the epicurean epitome of Texas. He asked of Raven, "Ya think old Judge Roy will be a-lookin' down on us?"

"Hush!" Raven replied, "I don't think the 'Law West of the Pecos' was concerned much with entertainment."

"Concerned!" responded Coyote, "That's *all* he was interested in! Remember the Bear? The cookouts? The hanging parties? The boxing match held on a sandbar in the middle of the river? Why, every session of his court was pure theatre. He even renamed this dust spot of a town, originally called Eagle Nest, after the singer, Lily Langtry."

It always irked Raven when Coyote was right. Raven tended to remember things through their highs and lows, in black and white, viewing the bigger picture. Coyote only seemed to remember the shades of grey, the details, not seeing the beginning or the end. Without that, thought Raven, how could one learn the lessons needed to be learned? Details were meaningless in the greater scheme of things.

Raven said, "You just be sure the sound system works through the night, not like in Presidio. I don't know if we'll ever be able to show our faces there, again."

"No great loss." muttered Coyote under his breath.

"What? And have the bus ready. As soon as the concert's over, I want to shift sand."

"Jawol, Mein Heir!" was the whispered response.

"What are you saying?" asked Raven.

"Nothin'! We'll be ready and everything will go just peachy keen." said Coyote.

Raven cocked and eye and looked at Coyote.

Coyote said, "Have I ever let you down?"

Raven opened his mouth but before he could utter a sound Coyote said, "Never mind!"

as told to Doug Hodges

Clouds had been gathering; the darkening sky promising one of the area's rare but powerful gully washers. Nonetheless, the small, single-roomed structure was packed. It could have once been a school, a barn, a grange hall, a church, even a saloon, but all trace of identification was gone. The unpainted wooden walls were now plastered with beer and tobacco ads as well as posters promoting An Unkindness Of Ravens. The band was tuning and warming up but could hardly hear themselves over the din of the crowd.

Thunder rumbled as the band swung into the first song. Midway through the third, flashes of lightning began an accompanying light show. With the next, a cowboy version of *Won't You Come Home Bill Bailey*, rain fell; an instantaneous deluge falling upon the roof. By the time the song was over, it was obvious that the roof leaked.

Water began to trickle down the beams and run along the rafters. There were perhaps only two or three real holes where buckets, had there been any, would have been nice. But the building was no longer dry and getting wetter.

A couple of the bands members were looking nervous, mainly the Raven on keyboard and Coyote who stood beside a black box with about dozen plugs and wires emerging, going off in all directions. It wasn't long before the Raven on bass and the lead guitar were also rolling their eyes and hurrying the beat. Raven, microphone in hand, was oblivious to it all as he sang and gyrated across the stage and back.

Then the inevitable happened. The bass player lit up like a Christmas tree. With a long drawn out, agonizing G, he froze, then flopped over on his back, the wire extending from his guitar sparking like a fuse.

The lead guitarist was gone, his instrument rocking on the floor, as was the drummer; the keyboardist's hands seemed glued to the board. Raven was oblivious and sang on. Coyote turned, took a step, and shouted, "Ohhh sh ..."

When the box he was running from exploded like the Fourth of July, he was slammed into and through one wall of the structure.

People were running everywhere; screaming and musical and not-so-musical notes mingled in the air with thunder. If anything, the noise was even greater than during the concert.

Yet, seemingly in a minute or so it was over. Raven stood alone upon the smoking stage, his feathers twisted and ruffled. The rest of

The Voice of Coyote

the building was empty. Coyote crawled back through the hole he had made. Not a bad silhouette, he thought. The band was gone, probably back at the bus. They never hung around when things went wrong.

Coyote said to Raven, "It's stopped raining!"

Raven said, "Wow!"

Coyote continued, "I don't suppose we'll get paid for this one, either."

Raven said, "Wow!"

Afterwards, in the bus, moving south along the Rio Grande, the Pecos River behind them, Coyote, driving, said, "You know Paul Newman had that twinkle in his eye. Judge Roy Bean never had that."

"No!" replied Raven. "Bean looked a little more like the Edgar Buchanan version."

"But," said Coyote, raising a paw, "Walter Brennan was the closest to capturing that double-edged sword personality."

"Amen!" said Raven as he closed his eyes to fall asleep.

August 29, 2002

as told to Doug Hodges

War Clouds

Coyote and Raven sat in the shade of a large cactus, out on the Great American Desert, in far western Texas. Great clouds were rolling and darkening off to the east, clouds of war.

"And what of war?" asked Raven of Coyote. "What do you think of war?"

Coyote responded, "I think nothing of war; a conundrum, an enigma wrapped in a riddle, one more pointless thing that humans do."

"Ahhh!" spoke Raven. "But, it is a glorious time. Great armies shining brightly in the sun, marching to violent and bloody destruction … a great mass of emotion and zeal, fervent righteousness, religious justification."

"Together as comrades," Raven went on, striding back and forth, warming to one of his favorite topics, "they charge into the very jaws of death; dauntless, fearless. Yes, I am kept busy as such times. The Valkyres sing. It is a grand time!"

"Not for the dying, I'm sure." said Coyote. "Or the maimed, the mothers, wives, family. I'm sorry, Raven, I just don't buy it!"

Coyote went on, "I see only wanton destruction, stupidity, and waste. Waste of life, technology, emotion … better used …"

"In what?" interrupted Raven. "A mundane existence of non-fulfilling years, of scraping out a living, of working at pointless, tedious, often hazardous and hateful jobs for little or no recognition. Only to slide a little less further down the ladder to obscurity.

"How cynical you are, Raven!" responded Coyote. "There is love, the raising of children and grandchildren, music and life ... each day a wonderful mystery to be explored and experienced … as the Great Spirit intended."

"And you, Coyote," spoke Raven, "are a dreamer, an idealist. God intended Man to be great, awesome, to live and die in a blaze of glory, like the martyrs sent down. The world is not a peaceful garden."

"But it is!" exclaimed Coyote. "All one has to do is live it that way. Once can choose to live your bellicose way, or any way at all. But, why live in depravation, in fear and paranoia? Why have your peak moments of existence be ones of violence?"

The Voice of Coyote

"Physically," Coyote went on, "one must accept and deal with what the Great Spirit deems to give them. Then, in their Spirit, their heart, their soul, they are as free as they may choose to be. They will be as in harmony, as in love, as at peace as they, themselves, choose. The Great Spirit gives the path; all other spirits, Man, you and I, choose how we follow it. Unfortunately, so many just don't know that."

"A pretty speech, Coyote!" Raven shook his head. "But, really no one wants to be free. They want to be led, to be taken care of, united in one family with one purpose, and be told what they think they want to hear. What other reasons have religion and government? Now, war is the best tool for all of this. Why do you think it visits Man so often?"

"It is sad!" said Coyote.

"It is glory! ... life, blood, and death ... Man's destiny!" Raven screamed.

"Then," Said Coyote softly, "I truly am grateful that I am not a Man. It gives me a headache in my heart just to think on it." And with that, Coyote was up and went leaping off into the sunset of the western Texas desert.

With each leap, the further he got away from Raven, the better he felt. He thought about the war clouds not at all.

for George W. Bush
October 8, 2002

as told to Doug Hodges

Coyote and The Prophet

Coyote arose from his bed, a sandy depression in the great western desert. He sang in the morning, giving thanks to the Great Spirit and all the Spirits of the four winds, in particular that of the South, from whence he, himself, came. Then he moved on, east, towards the great salt water.

He had just passed the settlement called Laredo whence he came upon a strange man. Dressed only in a long brown robe, tied with a piece of twine, the man's hair and beard were long, unkempt and wild.

"Behold," cried the man, raising his arms upward to the heavens, "it is the seventh hour of the seventh day and here we are, face to face with the demon, Coyote."

Coyote sat down and scratched an ear with a hind leg. "Am I a demon, then?" he asked. "I would think you more the demonic type than myself. Who are you, anyway?"

"I!" cried the man, seemingly rising in height, "I am the Prophet Ahab!"

"Ahab wasn't a prophet." Replied Coyote, "He was an evil King."

"Appointed by God, he was …" the man rambled, waving his arms about. "We all are … and we all serve as we are called. Ahab was given chance after chance to conquer his ghosts … I, too … but he failed … not once but many times … down throughout history … but now … now, I am come into my own, into the world … as God's vessel …"

"Uh, OK. Can't argue with that." Said Coyote. "But why call me a demon, oh prophet. The term does not have a good connotation."

"You are full of the old spirit." The Prophet pointed a long shaky finger. "You, your gods are dead! Christ has washed you away in His blood, the blood of the living God …"

"Excuse me!" interrupted Coyote. "I am Coyote. I exist, no more nor less than the wind. I am Spirit, but no more god than you. There is only one Great Spirit. Humans can call me a god or a demon and it makes no difference. I am merely what I am. I can't help how you humans perceive me."

The Voice of Coyote

Coyote felt himself warming up, "You humans tend to make too much of things. The rain is the rain; an earthquake is an earthquake. Gods, or even God, doesn't make them happen. Things ... just are!"

"Humans don't need Prophets, like yourself, to tell them about things, what they have meant, what they mean, what they will mean. There's enough innate paranoia in the human spirit, already. It doesn't need to be fueled even more."

"Ahh, haa!!" cried the man. "Get thee behind me Satan! You are a disbeliever! You would divert me from my course!"

Coyote sighed, "We all have our own path. I would no more try to dissuade you from yours than I would wish you to try to dissuade me from mine." Which of course you would without thinking, said Coyote to himself. "A good day to you!"

The wild man stared bug-eyed as Coyote moved on down the path; he rent his garments even more, beat upon his breast and made the sign of the cross. "I will pray for your soul!", he shouted.

But Coyote was no longer there to hear and the voice died in the silence of the desert.

January 16, 2003

as told to Doug Hodges

The Faithful Companion, Coyote

i

Once upon a time, two riders made their way across the barren and arid wastes of the west. The first rode a snow-white stallion and was a figure all in black. This was Raven. Above his beak he wore a black domino mask which could scarcely be seen against the black of his face.

At his side, and a little behind, upon a painted pony, rode Coyote.

The two had just peaked a sandy knoll when the sound of gunfire split the air.

"That way, Coyote!" exclaimed Raven and he was off in a black and white blur. Coyote followed through a cloud of dust.

Ahead and slightly below them, a stagecoach was racing madly down the road, trailing, and almost encompassed in, a massive dust cloud. It rocked this way and that and the two right wheels left the ground as it careened wildly around a left turn.

Pursuing the stage were a half dozen riders, all riding bay horses, and all with forty-fives in their hands, blazing away.

"Desert Rats, Coyote!" shouted the masked Raven. "Faster!"

Coyote followed through the dust from the white stallion's feet, now mingled with the dust from the Rat's horses, and that of the stage, itself.

Two huge black revolvers appeared in Raven's hands. Blam! Blam! Two of the Rats fell from their mounts. The others looked over their shoulders.

"It's The Raven!" exclaimed one who appeared to be the leader. "Vamonos, muchachos!" And the four remaining rats rode off in four different directions firing a few futile final shots back over their shoulders.

The stage pulled to a stop in a mushroom cloud of dust. Lathered horses panted. The stage company men were Bears. The driver, looking wan and pale, held one hand to a bloody shoulder. The guard lay limp and dead, half on and half off of the top of the stage.

The Voice of Coyote

"Sure a good thing ya happened along, Raven." said the driver. "I thought we was gonners f'good."

Raven dismounted and opened the stage door. "Everyone all right in there?" he asked.

"There's only I!" said a small voice and Rabbit descended.

"That's right, Raven." said the driver. "Jes Miss Rabbit, the mail, and the strongbox this trip."

"Well, we'll round up the bodies and see you safely into town." said Raven. "Coyote, fetch those varmints here. Their horses shouldn't be far off."

Coyote, who had dismounted and was wiping dust from the face of his horse and himself, said, "Si!"

"Oh, and tend to the driver will ya. He seems to be injured. I'll look after Miss Rabbit." And Raven led the shaken but brave young lass to the shade of a nearby rock outcropping. The driver fainted and fell off the seat to the ground with a dusty thud.

Coyote sighed and walked over to him.

In short time, Coyote had the driver bandaged, watered and looking almost alive on top of the stage. The stage horses had been rested and watered; the two Rat outlaws, ornery looking scuds, tied across the saddles of their rested and watered horses.

Coyote brushed at his buckskins. "Hokay, Kemozombe, we's ready!"

"Ahh," said Raven, "Excellent! Miss Rabbit, allow me to help you up." And with all in place, they headed down the road to town.

Town was Buffalo Wallow, a dip in the road offering some dozen structures, three streets, a general store, a livery stable, a hotel, Marshal's Office and jail, three saloons, and various attendant businesses and homes.

The caravan pulled up in front of the Stage Office which happened to be next to the Marshal's Office.

"Oh, ho! What's this?" cried a big fellow wearing a tin star on his left breast.

"Stage was held up." said the driver. "The Raven here drove 'em off. And, made fer two of 'em."

The Marshal looked up at Raven with steely eyes, "So, you drove 'em off, huh? Mighty coincidental you bein' there, in the right place, at the right time, so to speak."

Raven stared back down at him, "Yes, it was."

as told to Doug Hodges

The Marshal turned his stare to Coyote. "We don' much like your kind around here."

Raven spoke up again, "He's with me."

"Don't you go getting all riled up at the wrong fellers, Marshal!" demanded Rabbit's small voice and she pushed her way in front. "These brave men risked their lives to save us. They're heroes and should be rewarded, not browbeaten."

"Now, Miss Rabbit, I ain't browbeatin' no one. But, as Marshal, it's my job to be suspicious."

While the two were arguing, Raven sidled over to Coyote, "Go check in the saloons and see if you can learn anything about the Rats."

"Raven," whined Coyote, "you know how these people are, 'Oh, look, there's Coyote, string 'em up!' 'Let's stomp the sh—- out o' him!'"

"Now, Coyote," placated Raven, "ya know that can't happen in ev'ry town."

And he was off to rescue Miss Rabbit from the Marshal.

'Yeah,' thought Coyote, 'not *ev'ry* town.'

ii

Night found Coyote sitting at a small table, in a dark, dingy corner of a dingier bar, listening. At a nearby table, four rats were playing cards; a big one looked suspiciously familiar to Coyote.

A voice was saying, "Oh, man, we almost had it. All them shiny sparklies in that box. That dang Raven, anyhow!"

"Hush! Ya wanna get us hung. We killed that guard."

"Yeah, but I just love shiny things like gold and silver and jewels and baubles."

"So do we all. We're Rats, ain't we. But, we gotta be careful with that blankety-blank Raven around."

"Hey, ain't that that dang Coyote in the corner there? I bet he's been listnin' to everythin' we've said."

Coyote started to get that sinking feeling.

"It sure is!" said the large Rat. "But, we can get rid of him."

"Hey!" the Rat stood up and shouted, pointing at Coyote. "It's a Coyote! I thought we had run all them out o' the territory. No wonder we've got crime back."

The Voice of Coyote

By this time, everyone in the bar had gathered around and things were looking ugly. Coyote sat in his chair, trying to be as invisible as possible.

"I think we should string him up." One of the Rats kicked over Coyote's table, grabbed him by the front of his shirt, raised him up and shook Coyote with both hands. "Who's got a rope."

"Yeah!" screamed the crowd. "Hang the Coyote! Hang the Coyote!"

'Son of a ...' thought Coyote. 'This is always happenin'. When am I gonna learn?'

The crowd swept up Coyote and with rope in hand, swept out the swinging doors of the saloon. "To the stable and the hanging beam!"

Meanwhile, Raven and Rabbit were having a quiet dinner in the restaurant of the hotel. "You know," spoke Raven, "My mask is not to hide any particular identity, rather to make me an anonymous crime fighter."

Rabbit looked closely, "Oh, you are wearing a mask, aren't you!" she exclaimed.

Hearing the din outside, Rabbit called to the waiter, "What on earth is going on outside?"

"Oh, dey found a Coyote in da bar an' der' goin' to string 'em up in da livery stable."

"Oh, my goodness!" said Rabbit. She thought to herself, 'Why is it always at my stable?'

"Not again!" sternly spoke Raven. "Will they never learn?"

"Oh," said the waiter, "it's just a Coyote. This sure ain't the first and I can tell ya it probably won't be the last."

Raven arose, "It'll be the last if I have anything to say about it." Placing his black hands on the black butts of his black revolvers to make sure they were loose, he strode purposely out of the restaurant.

In the stable, a single massive beam ran the full length of the building. From it, over the open center of the stable was tied a rope. Directly under this was a wagon with a horse hitched. Standing on the flat bed of the wagon, hands tied behind him, a noose around his neck, stood Coyote.

He was standing on the balls of his feet, the wagon bed moving with the nervousness of the horse. He was thinking, 'This gets very old. Each time I say, never again ...'

as told to Doug Hodges

The Marshal said, "Boys, ya cain't do this! We got no evidence he done anythin' wrong. Besides, he's the masked guy's friend."

"What do we care? He's a Coyote, ain't he? The only good Coyote's a dead ..."

Ka-blamm!

The rope above Coyote's head parted and he fell with a grunt to the bed of the wagon. 'Never again!' he thought.

"I'm ashamed of you folks!" cried Raven. "This is a free country, governed by laws, guaranteeing all individuals truth and justice. If Coyote has committed a crime, charge him. Bring him to trial. Let a jury of his peers convict him. Then hang him. That's justice!"

Coyote had shaken off his bonds and stood looking at Raven. 'He gets more and more off each time,' he thought. 'I gotta find a new game!'

The crowd was lickered and ugly. It was them, some twenty strong, against one man. The Marshal stood indecisively aside. The Rats knew they still had the upper hand.

"He's just one Man!" screamed the large Rat. "We all know that Coyotes are no good! Why does The Raven wear a mask? What's he hiding?"

The crowd responding with a "Yeah!!" to each jibe.

Raven spoke, "You don't go there, pardner!"

"Take him!" the Rat shouted. The crowd surged forward.

Blam, Blam went Raven's guns. Two coal oil lamps exploded showering flame upon the insurgents. Like cattle, the crowd panicked and headed for the front doors, trampling each other underneath.

Raven grabbed Coyote by the arm and rushed him out a side door, "The horse are out back."

There stood Rabbit beside the two waiting mounts, "Oh Raven! I'm sorry it had to be like this."

"Me, too." said Raven, "Some people never learn."

He took Rabbit in his arms, kissed her on the lips, then mounted the great white stallion.

Coyote, already mounted, looked down at Rabbit. He said, patiently, "It's always like this."

Then the two rode away into the night.

A night lit by the flaming torch of Rabbit's burning stable.

2/22/03

The Voice of Coyote

what can I sing of?
so early in the morning
of the birth of the sun
of the renewed day
the birds need not think
but are a spontaneous chorus

Doug Hodges

Coyote Illustrations:

Page 4 comes from a vintage post card – 1939, c. J.C. Haberstroh, Sanborn Souvenir Co., Denver, CO; "227 – The Call of the Wild, Coyote Barking at the Moon."

Page 92 comes from two vintage post cards – 1944, E.C. Kropp Co., Milwaukee, WI; "The Call of the Wild, Coyote Barking at the Moon – M19," & 1936, c. A.J. Luke, Luke & Co., Ft. Worth, TX; "Coyote Howling at Night near Uvalde, TX."

The cover illustration and Page 105 come from a vintage post card – "Call of the Wild – A Nevada Coyote."

The back cover photograph was taken by my wife, Linda Rubio, of Brownsville, TX
February, 2003.

as told to Doug Hodges

The Voice of Coyote

as told to Doug Hodges

About The Author

Doug Hodges was raised in the foothills of the Colorado Rockies. He worked for a series of four newspapers spanning twenty-one years.

As a result of a Quest, in Big Bend, TX, in 1998, Doug quit his job, sold most of what he owned, and took to the road.

Here, he was given tales, songs, and images to record and share.

He presently lives in the Rio Grande Valley where he has married, and still records images, songs, and tales.

Printed in the United States
1250000003B/448-522